Praise for Amanda Cross and her Kate Fansler novels

"No one has a sharper eye than Amanda Cross."
—*The Washington Post Book World*

"Cross is wise in the ways of academe, and her figures speak in literate, complete sentences, which surely is a requirement for nuanced ambiguity."
—*The Boston Globe*

"Treat yourself to some of the best mysteries around, and read all the Kate Fansler novels. You won't be disappointed."
—*Bay Area Reporter*

"Cross remains queen of the American literary whodunit."
—*Publishers Weekly*

By Amanda Cross:

*Published by The Ballantine Publishing Group

THE THEBAN MYSTERIES

Amanda Cross

Fawcett Books • New York
The Ballantine Publishing Group

Published by The Ballantine Publishing Group

Copyright © 1971 by Carolyn G. Heilbrun
Copyright renewed 1999 by Carolyn G. Heilbrun

All rights reserved under International and Pan-American Copyright Conventions. Published in the United States by The Ballantine Publishing Group, a division of Random House, Inc., New York, and simultaneously in Canada by Random House of Canada Limited, Toronto. Originally published by Alfred A. Knopf, a division of Random House, Inc.

Fawcett is a registered trademark and the Fawcett colophon is a trademark of Random House, Inc.

www.randomhouse.com/BB/

A Library of Congress Catalog Card Number can be obtained from the publisher upon request.

ISBN 0-449-00706-5

Manufactured in the United States of America

First Ballantine Books Edition: April 2001

10 9 8 7 6 5 4 3 2 1

To **IMΦ**
and **ΠO**

No, *though a man be wise, 'tis no shame for him to learn many things, and to bend in season.*

—ANTIGONE

One

THE telephone and the front doorbell rang simultaneously in the Amhearst apartment with a call to action which, Reed happily observed, reminded him of plays like *You Can't Take It With You*.

"Those were good days in the theater," he said, rising from the couch where he and Kate were enjoying a cocktail.

"Perhaps," Kate answered, putting down her glass, "but I can't help feeling that the Greeks wrote great plays because they got the characters on and off the stage without the aid of bells."

"You get the door," Reed said. "I'll get the telephone." He walked down the passage to his study and lifted the receiver. "Hello," he said, wishing he had thought to bring his martini with him.

"This is Miss Tyringham of the Theban," a woman's

cultured voice greeted him on the phone. "May I please speak to Mrs. Reed Amhearst?"

"This is Mr. Amhearst of Kaufman and Hart," Reed wanted ridiculously to answer. He could hear Kate at the door. "Oh, my God!" he heard her say in astonished tones which boded no good. "Well, come in for a time anyway, and let's talk about it."

"Can you hold on for a moment?" Reed asked. "I'll see if she's available."

"Thank you. I do apologize for disturbing you at this hour, but it is a matter of some importance. Mrs. Amhearst was Kate Fansler, was she not, when she was at the Theban?"

Was, is, and ever more will be, Reed happily thought. "Yes," he answered. "Hold on a moment."

He made his way back into the living room cautiously, as a cat might return to a place invaded by unknown, perhaps dangerous, beings.

He found Kate mixing herself another martini—in itself an ominous sign, since she always claimed that when Reed mixed them they were nectar, and when she mixed them they were intoxicating hair oil—while collapsed on the couch, its head in its hands, was a long-haired youth, revealing himself by his beard as male and by the fact that he rose, after a moment's hesitation, to his feet as having, in some dimly remembered era, been taught the manners of a lost world. On the run, Reed thought. Let us hope it *is* Kaufman and Hart, not Sophocles.

"Reed," Kate said, "may I introduce John Megareus Fansler, known as Jack to his friends."

"Of whom he has many, I'm sure," Reed said, holding out a hand.

"That," Kate said, "is Philip Barry."

"A nephew?" Reed asked. "Related to that other nephew, Leo? I don't believe we've met."

"You haven't," Kate said. "Jack did not appear at that massive family reception given by the Fanslers for us newlyweds. Clever him."

Jack smiled. "Leo told me it was pretty hairy," he said, "except for the food. Ted, who is only twelve, never notices anything *but* food. My brothers."

"Will you have a drink?" Reed asked, bending over the martini pitcher. "Beer, perhaps? Sherry?"

Jack shook his head. "I don't drink," he said. "I don't want anything."

"I always forget that your generation doesn't drink," Reed said. "Nor," he added, rising from mixing his martini, "should my generation. I've forgotten the formidable lady on the phone, asking for Kate Fansler that was. She has probably decided you no longer are, and has gone away."

But, when Kate picked up the receiver, Miss Tyringham was still there. Kate apologized.

"It is I who should apologize for disturbing you at this hour," Miss Tyringham said. "I'm calling at the suggestion of Julia Stratemayer. Did Mr. Amhearst tell you this is Miss Tyringham, headmistress of the Theban?"

At the name the Theban there rushed through Kate's mind, instantaneously as is supposed to happen when one is drowning, a whole series of recollections: singing "Holy, Holy, Holy" at the opening assembly, the elevators in which one was not supposed to talk, profound discussions of sex in the john, the line in the cafeteria, persuading her parents not to send her away to boarding school. "I don't believe," Miss Tyringham continued, "that we have met."

"No," Kate said. "But I gather from Julia Stratemayer that you are all coping, in these difficult times."

"We try, but it isn't easy. One never knows what will turn up, all the girls in pants, or in sandals, or barefoot, or wanting to close the school because of the war. We try to move with events, which come not singly but in battalions. Julia is doing a wonderful job on the revised curriculum."

"So I hear," Kate said. She wondered where the conversation could possibly be leading. Miss Tyringham, though she had been twenty years in the school, had come after Kate's graduation. She had the reputation of being a first-rate head, but Kate, apart from an idle glance at the alumnae bulletin, a willing response to alumnae fund-raising pleas, and delightful conversations about the Theban with her friend and classmate Julia Stratemayer, thought of her school as in another world.

"Has Julia perhaps anticipated my call and told you all about it?"

"No. All about what?"

"We are in a jam," Miss Tyringham said. "One of the curriculum changes already instituted is that which allows the seniors to spend their final semester in small seminars on subjects of their own choice. All their requirements have been fulfilled, and we are trying to prevent the final semester from being anticlimactic, particularly since that semester's work does not count for college admissions. Are you still there?"

4

"Still here," Kate said. "I remember about the last semester, though of course in my day one pretended to be working while not."

"Yes. No one pretends anything any more, which I suppose is a good thing, though I can't help sometimes feeling that the constant expression of emotion in itself becomes the cause of the emotion which is expressed. But that is neither here nor there. One of the senior seminars is a study, with all possible modern ramifications, of the *Antigone* of Sophocles."

"Well," Kate said, "that sounds properly scholarly and irrelevant."

"Only at first blush. Antigone stands, you see, for expressions of love versus tyranny, for actions of a woman against a male-dominated world, for the battles of youth against age. I understand that George Eliot was particularly intrigued with the *Antigone*, which is perhaps what suggested you to Julia Stratemayer."

"I'm delighted to be brought to mind by the thought of George Eliot," Kate said, "but I'm afraid I don't altogether . . ."

"Of course you don't; I'm being frightfully long-winded. Mrs. Johnson, who was to have done the seminar, has slipped a disc. She must be flat on her back and in traction for months. The new semester, of course, begins next week. Julia, knowing how *desperately* we needed someone frightfully exciting to take over the seminar, suggested . . ."

"But Miss Tyringham," Kate interrupted. "I'm on leave this year."

"Exactly, my dear. We thought—rather we hoped—that therefore you would have the time. The girls are really *very* keen, but they do require a teacher who is not only experienced in the running of seminars but also, as they would say, 'with it.' Unfortunately most classicists, while terribly sound on the study of Greek, do not always appreciate the modern ramifications in quite the way we might hope. Mrs. Amhearst, we are in desperate need of help, and appeal to your charity and kindness. Of course we will pay, but I realize . . ."

"May I have a little time to think about it?" Kate asked. "You see, I'm supposed to be working on a book."

"Oh, I know you're frightfully busy and will have to squeeze us in. I can't express how grateful we would be. Now, don't say anything yet. I'll ask Mrs. Johnson to send you her reading list; perhaps you would like to talk to her. I'll give you a day or two to decide. Shall I call you in a few days, Mrs. Amhearst?"

"All right. Miss Tyringham, I hope you don't mind, but professionally, and you do want a professional I take it, I use the name Kate Fansler. Miss Fansler, if the students still call their teachers by their last names."

"Good for you. Of course, my dear. One wants to be correct socially, but no one knows better than the head of a girls' school how confusing this continual change of names can be, particularly in these days of frequent divorce and remarriage. Goodbye for now, Miss Fansler, and I hope, indeed I trust, that you will come to our aid in this emergency."

Kate's goodbye echoed faintly over the already disconnected line. Swearing, she quickly dialed Julia Stratemayer's number. "Julia," Kate said, when she had got her friend on the telephone, "I have just heard from Miss Tyringham, and if I were not at the moment occupied with a troubled nephew, I would come over and wring your neck."

"Listen, Kate," Julia said, "I know how you feel, but I honestly think you'll find these seniors fascinating, and anyway we're desperate."

"The *Antigone*, Julia, I ask you. I haven't thought about Greek since the Theban."

"Never mind Greek, love; read the play with the aid of Jebb. Virginia Woolf thought there hadn't been a real woman character between Antigone and her own Mrs. Ramsay. And George Eliot . . ."

"I will not discuss George Eliot without another drink. And then there's Jack. Can we," Kate frantically concluded, "thrash this out tomorrow?"

Back in the living room, Kate found Reed and Jack making conversation. The boy, having learned of Reed's association with the D.A.'s office, was accusing him of being part of the oppressive police force, an arm of the Establishment, a tool of the system. Reed declined, however, to rise to the bait. He could clearly discern that the boy was troubled, and he did not wish, should his help be needed, to put the boy into the position of having to refuse it.

"Good news, I hope," he said to Kate.

"That," Kate said, "was the head of the Theban. Girlhood memories dance before my eyes."

"Miss Tyringham," Jack said. "She and the head of my old school keep talking about combining."

"Why on earth?" Kate asked.

"To be coed, of course."

"My God," Kate said. "But then, I suppose if

Haemon and Antigone had been to school together, it might have been a different story."

"Babble on," Reed said.

"Kate," Jack said. He pulled on his beard in a gesture Kate found odd in so young a man. "Dad's thrown me out. And I've quit Harvard. Could you lend me a little money till I get a job?"

"Jack dear, you will bear in mind, will you not, that your father is my brother? True, I have often disagreed with him; in fact, I can't remember ever having agreed with him about anything. But I don't feel comfortable going behind his back. Does he know you're here?"

"He doesn't know or care where I am."

"Would you mind if I told him you were here?"

"If that fits in with your straight way of doing things, go ahead. He will merely mention my juice and me stewing in it."

"What's happened?"

"I'm going to sign up with my draft board as a C.O. I guess hearing that did it. My hair, I mean, and quitting Harvard, and now this. I don't believe in this filthy war."

"Does your father want you to be in it?"

"He wouldn't mind using his connections to get me into a cushy slot at the Pentagon; I don't suppose he'd object to my pulling a high number in the lottery. What he can't stand is what he calls my spitting on the flag— you can find his opinion expressed alliteratively by Agnew. The way I look at it, if you don't protest against war you're going along with it. I could even probably get out because of my asthma, but that wouldn't let them know how I feel about Vietnam, would it? Leo wanted to come with me, but I told him to stick with school till he's eighteen. He thinks you're great."

Kate looked at Reed. "Any suggestions?" she asked.

"Call your brother. I'll broil a steak we can all have for dinner. All right with you, Jack?"

"Right on," Jack said.

Two

THE Theban School was a hundred years old, and had been founded by Matthias Theban because he wanted a school in which properly to educate his four daughters. Other men might have thrown up their hands, hired governesses, and cursed a fate which had deprived them of a son. Such was not Matthias Theban's way. If fate had presented him with female progeny, he would accept fate's challenge and educate them as human beings and future members of the learned professions. Combining as he did an eccentric view of the possible destiny of females with a great deal of money, influence, and financial acumen, he was able, in those simpler days, to carry out his plan with an ease which must seem the stuff of daydreams to those who try to found any institution today. Matthias Theban had no need to consult bureaucracies, local governments, foundations, or minority groups. He bought a piece of

11

real estate in downtown New York in a section he was fairly certain would increase in value, persuaded influential friends onto his board of trustees, hired a forward-looking educator from Harvard (a man; but it was Matthias Theban's hope, not realized until the twentieth century, to have a woman as head of the Theban), built his school, and got his educational experiment under way.

In the years which followed, New York saw the establishment of many girls' schools, some new boys' schools, and a number of schools which were coeducational—although these tended to be more experimental and less aristocratic. Spence, Chapin, Brearley, Miss Hewitt's, Nightingale-Bamford, and Sacred Heart joined the Theban in the group which came to be known as the "curtsying sisters": their students curtsied when introduced to an adult, shook hands properly, wore uniforms topped by a school blazer, and were accepted, almost on application, by the college of their choice. All this, of course, was before the middle of the twentieth century. By then, no one over ten curtsied, shook hands, or wore a uniform without protest, and acceptance by a college required as extended and difficult a procedure as the acquisition of Swiss citizenship. The Theban, though one of the curtsying sisters, was nonetheless special, as all its graduates knew with a calm certainty particularly aggravating to graduates of any other school. What made the Theban special was hard to define, though many people, Kate among them, had tried. It imbued its students, despite their inevitable destiny of cotillions and debuts, with a tomboy, bluestocking attitude which was never entirely eschewed.

The Theban boasted (a figure of speech: the Theban never boasted about anything) several gyms into which the girls, at odd though scheduled hours, would fling themselves to play basketball, volleyball, or indoor baseball, to high jump or swing wildly, like monkeys, across the ceiling on rings. The Theban was usual in requiring four years of Latin, unusual in offering three years of Greek. It paid unusually high faculty salaries, and taught its students so thoroughly that all of them, to a woman, found college an anticlimax of almost unmanageable proportions. The average Theban girl (though no Theban girl was ever average) discovered two weeks after she had arrived at Vassar or Radcliffe that she could get A's with no effort whatever; she settled down, therefore, to three years of bridge, love affairs, and an occasional nervous breakdown, pulling herself sufficiently together in her senior year to graduate with honors and move on, if she chose, to graduate school. Many Theban girls chose, and the school's alumnae rolls were impressive indeed, or would have been had the Theban published them. But the Theban had no interest in impressing anyone.

At its founding, the Theban had been unique in yet another way: it had accepted Jews. Only the right Jews, of course, the ones who were one day to be dubbed "our crowd"; nonetheless, in this as in other actions, Matthias Theban was far ahead of his day. The school's graduating classes were sprinkled with Warburgs, Schiffs, Loebs, and Guggenheims; later, after the Second World War, when even Spence, Chapin, and Miss Hewitt's felt the need to welcome a few Jews, the Theban found itself to have been revolutionary without ever losing its reputation for conservatism: a neat trick.

But not so neat as combining educational wisdom with the finer points of real-estate speculation. The Theban's first building, by the time it had been outgrown and the neighborhood had become too commercial, was sold for many times what it had cost: the profits built the new building and swelled the endowment fund. After Matthias Theban's death, the school once again called his name blessed: their second building, standing on the spot now occupied by the Biltmore, easily paid for the third and current home of the school in the East Seventies.

Kate had been in the lower school of the Theban at the end of the Depression, the middle school during World War II, the upper school during the Cold War and the frenzied return to normal. Through all these cataclysms the Theban stood firm and steady. It made its concessions, of course: even for the Fanslers, the Guggenheims, and the Rockefellers there were concessions to be made. But nothing essential changed. Kate left the Theban before the fifties, when all over the country students, called "the silent generation," conformed; a demagogue reduced the nation to a gaggle of witch hunters; and upper-class young ladies moved to the suburbs, had several children, and talked about their feminine role.

It was Miss Tyringham who kept the Theban alive in the fifties. She took no political stands—such was not the policy of Theban heads. But she confirmed, in her downright, cheerful way, that change was possible. She knew that schools do not die; they pass from being vigorous to being fossils without ever noticing the transition. This passage Miss Tyringham prevented before anyone else had considered it. She subtly altered the school's acceptances away from the predominance of old money toward those who were nouveaux riches enough still to be vigorous. Naturally she made some mistakes, and the Theban graduated the occasional girl more vulgar than one might have wished; without risks, as she knew, there were no gains. Her faculty began to shift its average age from fifty-five to thirty-five; she encouraged the hiring of young married women, encouraged them to teach through their pregnancies, found substitutes for them during their deliveries, and cheered them upon their early return. She added contemporary literature and history to the curriculum long before that became fashionable, introduced Spanish as an alternative language to French in a city now heavily Puerto Rican, recruited for the school numbers of black girls, and bullied the trustees into providing scholarships for them—all before Martin Luther King had begun boycotting the buses in Montgomery. Honoring ideas from her faculty, she nurtured an extraordinary esprit de corps while most private schools, allowing a patina of chilly courtesy to form, unsuccessfully disguised from students the hostilities which divided the faculty into contending factions. Miss Tyringham was, in short, a genius at her job.

Yet not even an administrative genius could have been prepared for the last half of the sixties. Everyone was unprepared, but—some were less unprepared than others. As a whole, the private schools weathered the storm through the use of cautious blackmail: their waiting lists were long, the idea of public school unthinkable. A suggestion that if Johnny or Susy did not behave their parents had perhaps better look for a school more suitable to their child's needs usually sufficed to achieve some change in demeanor.

For a while. But, by 1968, some students were ready to fling out of school in spite of any threats, parental or scholastic. At the Theban, the esprit de corps held, for the most part. Miss Tyringham, firm and cheerful as ever, coped with pants in school (she ignored them), drugs (she gave the students and their parents the facts in the clearest, least moralistic way), the black revolution (she had foreseen that), and the demands for coeducation (in regular meetings with the headmaster of the boys' school Kate's nephews attended she explored the situation, emerging from time to time with enigmatic reports; whether she was considering coeducation or stalling, no one quite knew).

What she could not cope with was the Vietnam War. Whether the history of the United States would have been fundamentally different without that war is a question scarcely worth asking now. What Miss Tyringham knew was that it had driven apart the generations and political parties of the Theban as no other crisis had ever done. Students began shouting one another down in assembly, greatly offending the older faculty, who had always assumed the practice of Jeffersonian democracy, the right of everyone to be heard. On Moratorium Days, the students refused to come to school. Miss Tyringham kept the school open as a center for discussion and petition writing, for or against the war (but very few were for it). She had already begun a radical curriculum reform, with Julia Stratemayer in charge; the school carried on. But, like everyone else in the country during the early months of 1970, Miss Tyringham was feeling the strain. This was the situation into which Kate walked on a suspiciously mild February day, the sort that promises spring as beguilingly as an incurable philanderer promises fidelity.

"Well, we *are* glad to see you," Miss Tyringham said, welcoming Kate into the head's office. The holy of holies, Kate thought. She could remember having been there only three times during her student days. Once when, as a member of the student government, she had been called to an important conference to discuss, not whether the students should be allowed to run the school and hire the faculty, which was the sort of thing that came up now, but whether the students could be sufficiently interested in their own affairs to justify any student government at all. Then, she had been in the office with her parents to discuss her college application; Miss Tyringham's predecessor had managed, with infinite grace, to talk Kate's parents out of Vassar (where her mother had gone) as she had three years earlier helped Kate talk them out of Milton Academy. Kate mentioned the three visits to Miss Tyringham. "And here I am now," she added, "to discuss Antigone. Did you know that the President of Princeton wrote a book on the imagery in the *Antigone*? In quieter, bygone days, of course."

"Did he indeed? I hope he is not the last college president this country has who is capable of doing that. Do you know, we shall actually be sending some graduates to Princeton this year? What exciting times we live in, as I keep trying to persuade the older parents, who wonder, in all the rapid change, if they may not outlive the earth itself. Our oldest living graduate mentioned to me recently that in her youth there were no automobiles to speak of, and now we have gone to the moon. I could not help rejoining that in her youth the Long Island Railroad was somewhat speedier than it is today, and the letters were delivered in half the time. None of that's important, of course. What matters is that we are today a society that must, whether we want it or not, be willing to learn from the young. That's a bitter pill for most people my age to swallow."

"If we haven't anything to teach, why are we teaching?" Kate asked.

Miss Tyringham leaned back in her chair, looked upward, and smiled—a smile as beautiful as any Kate had ever seen. Miss Tyringham was, indeed, a beautiful woman, not the less so because her face, which had been ever free of makeup, her hair, which had always been casually brushed back, seemed trying to detract from her beauty, to deny it: the onlooker perceived the beauty more acutely because he imagined he had shown unusual perception in noticing it at all. There were, to be sure, those among the parents who objected to Miss Tyringham's way of "getting herself up," and they used occasionally to express to one another their wish that *someone* would tell her not to wear such mannish suits. The parents of girls who had *not* been accepted at the Theban made more pointed remarks about Miss Tyringham. Kate admired the courage or natural insouciance or simple shortage of time which permitted one to be so emphatically oneself.

"I wonder," Miss Tyringham said, "if our whole definition of the word 'teach' does not need to be reconsidered. Have we perhaps for too long supposed teaching to be a ritual in which I, the elder and supposedly wiser, hand on to you, the younger and more innocent, the fruits of my learning and experience? Perhaps teaching is really a mutual experience between the younger and older, perhaps all there is to be learned is what they can discover between them. I don't of course mean, as so many of the girls here clearly do, endless bull sessions where everyone talks and no one listens, let alone learns. I mean a disciplined sort of seminar in which one person, you for example, moderates, schedules, and referees, always in the expectation that you, like the students, will emerge with new insights into the *Antigone* none of you might ever have achieved alone."

"Well," Kate said, admiring the way her instructions had been so painlessly imparted, "there's certainly no danger of my posing as an authority on the life and habits of the Greeks—but you know, even were I an authority, most of the fruits of my learning would be readily available in paperback. I've become convinced that our old ideas of teaching date back to the days when there were so few books that only some priest had read them; he then passed on the information to the others, thirsting for knowledge but bookless. Which, no doubt, is why they are called lectures—now as applicable to our life as those hot academic gowns, designed for wear in drafty monasteries, in which we parade beneath a hot June sun. All the same, I hope you don't regret having asked me. I'm afraid of performing like a wallflower who, when asked to dance, can't think of a word to say to the man."

"You are hardly a wallflower in the academic world."

"In *this* academic world I am; they are so young, so certain, so self-absorbed. No doubt they must be, to survive adolescence. But I'm not sure that I understand their language, any more than I understand their dances."

"Not to put too fine a point on it," Miss Tyringham said, "you still have the weapons of marks and reports which go on their school records; anyway, all the old habits of diffidence have not wholly gone. But I do think there are new forms of dialogue, even within education. Hopeful speech for today."

"I'm glad you can still make hopeful speeches. Reed and I have been afflicted with a nephew—in fact, he and you entered our lives, so to speak, if not hand in hand, ring by ring. I had the delightful task of talking to Harvard, an institution whose reasons for continuing existence he seems to find remarkably scarce, apart, of course, from serving the military-industrial complex. Well, it turned out, as you no doubt can guess, that Harvard like every other college has had so many flights from the nest that they now have a code for unofficial leaves in their computers. Jack is to be allowed back with lots of concessions on *both* sides. Colleges may be hell to get into now, but apparently once they take you in they are admirably reluctant about pushing you out, or even letting you leave slamming the door behind you. Whether that's nobility or guilty conscience I'm quite unable to decide."

"*You* seem to have decided the main things, you, rather than the boy's parents. Usual, I'm afraid. Will he stay at Harvard?"

"Temporarily. What is troubling, Miss Tyringham, is that he is rude, unwashed, inconsiderate, filled to the brim with slogans, and outrageously simplistic. Alas, he is also right."

"About everything?"

"Hardly that. But he is right about my brother, right about this terrible war, and wonderfully courageous in a maddening way. I mean, we are all for principles in the abstract, but most of us will not turn down a perfectly good cop-out if it is ready to hand."

"That's called compromise."

"What the young will never do. Brave them. Well, brave me too. Do you mind if I look around? I may even sneak up to one of the gyms and swing from a rope."

"Mrs. Copland is waiting to show you around. I'm sure you would have liked Julia as tour guide, but she's at a meeting with some woman who comes once a week and lectures us all on computers—then I *do* long for the simpler days. You'll like Mrs. Copland, I think. She teaches literature to the elevens and is home-room teacher to the sixes. We're grooming her for the head of the English Department when she gets through having babies, but don't tell her because we don't want to scare her off. I've so much enjoyed talking with you," Miss Tyringham concluded, rising in her chair and vigorously shaking Kate's hand. "Remember, we don't have to wait for an emergency to have another chat."

Which God knows was true, they didn't have to wait for an emergency. Before too long they were overtaken by an emergency no one would have dreamed of waiting for.

Three

KATE, having declined the help of Miss Tyringham's secretary in finding Mrs. Copland, went in search of the room which held the sixes. The school, largely unchanged since Kate's day, was spacious enough, but dated. Nothing ages more quickly than the absolutely up-to-date. All new school buildings, boasting the latest in everything, age like a woman who has had her face lifted: there is not even character to set off the ravages of time. Still, one could scarcely set out to build oneself Winchester in New York City, could one?

Not liking to knock on a classroom door—as unsuitable as the knock of a trained British servant in the days of the Empire—Kate opened the door slowly.

"Ah," Mrs. Copland called from the front of the room. "Come in. We have just finished." Kate pushed the door all the way open and was greeted by the raucous sound of thirty chairs being pushed back and thirty twelve-year-olds rising to their feet. Kate looked horrified. "Sit down, ladies," Mrs. Copland said. "Let us see if you can stay in the study hall three minutes alone without tearing down the walls. The bell is about to ring." She followed Kate from the room, firmly closing the door behind her.

"Will there be an explosion?" Kate nervously asked.

"Not in three minutes. Welcome to the Theban. It's welcome back, isn't it?"

"I too rose to my feet in just that same way. Has anyone ever considered the effect it has on the unprepared adult who enters?"

"Only these days, because it's so unexpected. Twenty years ago, I understand," Mrs. Copland said, leading the way down the hall, "any adult not greeted by the sound of humble youth rising to its feet would have expired on the spot and had to be revived with sal volatile or whatever it was in the nurse's office. Shall we begin the tour on the top floor? I know you must remember everything, but Miss Tyringham felt that refreshment was in order. We are to discuss the problems of teaching literature on the way. Ah," she concluded as the elevator opened, "ten please. My name's Anne. I don't leap to the use of first names immediately as a rule, but I discovered that if one is going to discuss senior seminars and disaffected youth, one had better skip the usual steps to familiarity. Here we are." They stepped out into the auditorium, at the moment occupied only in the farthest corner by a group involved either in dramatics or an encounter session; which was not immediately clear.

The tenth and top floor of the Theban was given over

entirely to the huge auditorium, which was able to seat the entire school. There was a stage at one end which, while scarcely the miracle of theatrical devices that even small theaters have subsequently become, served very well for Theban performances, which tended, as in Greek and Shakespearean times, to emphasize the language and costumes rather than the scenery and lights. In front of the stage, at the moment, stood music stands, indicating to Kate that musical activities had not abated since her day, she having played the viola in a rather frantic string ensemble which was wont to present musical offerings from time to time.

The dramatic or encounter group now in session was in one of the corners of the auditorium farthest from the stage, no doubt to emphasize the spontaneity of their undertaking. Kate looked at them inquiringly.

"Something new," Anne Copland said. "A combination of dramatics, playwriting, and self-expression. I believe Mrs. Banister is new since your time; she's extremely popular with the girls, who no longer feel properly purged if they have merely acted Hedda Gabler with all the necessary passion. Those who take dramatics as an activity now write their own plays, or spontaneously allow them to erupt. Most interesting, really—sort of a combination of Samuel Beckett and group therapy. Perhaps we'll see Mrs. Banister at lunch—she's really most enthusiastic. With all the seats set up in here we're rather crowded now, since the school is at least two hundred girls larger than this building was intended for. But there's the most terrible need for schools, and Miss Tyringham and the trustees felt that we should meet our obligations."

Kate could see the seats piled up at the sides of the

stage; supposedly, there were more in some storage area beyond. She noticed two elevator doors, several doors marked STAIRS with red EXIT signs above them, and two small doors to the side of the stage.

"Were those always there?" Kate asked.

"Oh yes, I think so. One notices different things as an adult. One leads backstage to the storage rooms and the places where you work the lights—all that; the other leads to the caretaker's apartment."

"Surely that's new."

"Like so much else these tumultuous days. Twenty years ago, and all the years before for that matter, you closed the school, locked the door, and didn't give the place another thought till morning. That was in the dear, dead days. We had a lot of people breaking in, to steal expensive equipment and so on, but the coup de grâce came when a group of unruly boys—tautology, I know, but these were especially unruly—broke in and apparently pranced about with spiked boots on the gymnasium floors. I don't know if you've ever gone with any care into the economics of gym floors—well, neither have I, but I gather they did enough damage to cost ten thousand dollars in repairs. Ergo, Mr. O'Hara. He's got a great view, an extremely fashionable address, and a great taste for solitude, which is just as well since the problems of entertaining on the roof of an empty school building would seem to me to be insurmountable. Everyone was quite impressed when we first heard about Mr. O'Hara, but we all take him for granted now. He's a retired army man and therefore used to doing for himself."

" 'Holy, Holy, Holy,' " Kate hummed to herself,

" 'Lord God Almighty! Early in the morning our song shall rise to Thee.' No doubt we each have our favorite hymn. Is it still sung at every opening assembly the first day of school?"

"As long as I've been here. Though I believe that a year or two ago there was a suggestion, freely translated as a demand, that we sing 'We Shall Overcome' instead."

"What did Miss Tyringham do?"

"Sang them both. After all, Martin Luther King was a minister, so she didn't have much trouble talking everybody into *that*."

"Do you find her as extraordinary as I do?" Kate asked, wondering if this was an impolitic question on such short acquaintance.

"Absolutely marvelous. As though she had done it all, and been it all, and somehow understood everything. People of that quality have always been rare, but these days she seems, I sometimes think, unique. Do you want to examine the murky backstage depths, or shall we descend? And, if we descend, shall we take the elevator in a fast plunge, or do you want to take the stairs, peering your way down one floor at a time?"

"Let's walk if you don't mind," Kate said. "Not that I want to examine the place as though I were going to buy it. You know, a sort of casual once-over."

As they walked toward the doors marked STAIRS Kate eavesdropped a bit on the drama group, not too difficult since the young ladies had apparently reached a highly emotional point and their voices were raised either in argument or animated discussion, depending on how you cared to look at it. The stricture from Kate's day and earlier that no lady raised her voice except in song had gone, and a damn good thing too, Kate thought. My brothers and I might have something to say to each other now, if we hadn't been terrified of family arguments.

"What do you really want?" one actor declaimed. "What do you wish for yourself; if you had one wish, what would it be? Can you even say?" Her hand came forward in a questioning, demanding gesture.

"Mrs. Banister likes them to use their whole bodies," Anne Copland whispered. "*And* their whole voices, more's the pity. Still, no doubt it does them good."

"I wish to return to the fundamental elements of life. I wish to live in a small community, where we are not dependent on technology and packaging, but can feel our closeness to the earth. I wish . . ." The door closed behind Kate and Anne Copland, leaving the unexpressed wish hanging in the air where, Kate could not help feeling, it rightfully belonged.

Their descent was rapid and for Kate full of reminiscences which she did not trouble to express. What is more trying than other people's memories, unless it is other people's dreams? Little had changed. Lockers still lined the halls. The classrooms, such empty ones as they examined, bore evidence that this was the age of posters. "Make love not war" and "War is dangerous to children and other living things" were the most frequently seen. Kate was interested in one poster which showed a coffin, with a flag draped over it, and underneath the caption: The Silent Majority.

"That's righter than you might suppose," Kate said.

"Homer used the phrase 'the silent majority,' referring to the dead."

"The most extraordinary change here is never talked about at all," Anne Copland said. "Since your time, or long, long before that, I'm certain this school has always been largely Republican in sentiment; not reactionary, you understand, but sound and vaguely right wing. It astounds me how little real support there is for President Nixon, his policies, and particularly his Vice President, not only among the students but among their parents. And these girls represent some of the most prominent families in the country. Of course, the staff isn't supposed to argue politics with the students, but that's easier said than done, these days."

"After all, these girls largely represent the Eastern Establishment—the people Nixon never tried to get on his side. Do politics come up regularly, if one can call them politics?"

"The politics of survival, the girls call them—I forget who first made up that phrase. Some of the posters are pretty outspoken or downright vulgar. ('Make love not babies' caused a *great* deal of discussion a while back) and many of the staff wanted to outlaw them altogether, but Miss Tyringham insisted they were to stay up if they didn't actually express an obscenity. We are surrounded with Bob Dylan and the Beatles, but they make the girls feel at home, I guess. This floor, as you see, has student art, which seems to me to change very little over the years."

"Lord, yes," Kate said, looking around her. "A portrait of someone with snowflakes falling—I remember doing the same thing myself, having dropped some white paint on the face I was doing and not being able to get it off. *Some* things remain the same. And that," she added, "is the supply closet."

"So it is. A particularly feverish memory, I gather."

"Sad, really, though I still can't think of it without chuckling. I was in the middle school, and we had acquired a German math teacher of overpowering qualifications. A refugee, no doubt, from Hitler. He knew a great deal and might even have been able to explain it so that a group of giggling eleven-year-olds could understand. But he was unbearably pompous and moralistic, always fulminating against American spoiled youth in general, and our own lack of manners, brains, and attention in particular. As they would say today, he didn't relate to the group. One day he stomped out to get some paper for an exam that was to punish us for our sins, and as one being we floated out the door and locked him in the supply closet. Then we went back to the classroom and bent innocently and silently over our books. His screams eventually aroused someone in authority."

"What happened?"

"Oddly enough, nothing. We waited for the fearful summons, but it never came. He was out sick for a week, and then it was Christmas; we all felt so bad we chipped in to buy him a fruitcake. When we returned from the vacation we had a new math teacher, frightfully up-to-date, who kept one lesson ahead of us, understanding children rather than decimals. What monsters youngsters are. Yet, you know, we weren't really unkind, only bewildered."

Anne Copland showed Kate the seminar rooms,

newly decorated, and each holding a table surrounded by chairs, with bookcases around the walls. "To get rid of the classroom look, heaven forfend," Anne explained. "The surroundings turned out to be half the battle. You'll be in here." She opened the door of a room at the moment empty. A sign "Hurrah for Antigone" was spread across the wall, and below it was a poster with a poem:

> *Miss Kate Fansler, who is she,*
> *Expounder of* Antigone?
> *Will she hold forth like old Tiresias*
> *Propounding some established thesias?*
> *Or will she know, or learn like Creon,*
> *That we'll discuss what we agree on?*

"Well," Anne said, looking at Kate with some trepidation, "you are warned. I didn't know that would be there. Hope you aren't offended."

"Not offended," Kate said. "Terrified."

They debouched, Kate feeling somewhat stricken, onto the entrance floor. She was not only slightly offended, which she had denied, and terrified, which she had admitted, but also a bit angry. It's easy enough to talk about the delightful and honest young, she thought, until they get their fangs into you. Now, why didn't I tell Miss Tyringham, impressive though she be, to take her seminar on *Antigone* and jolly well teach it herself if she's such a bloody genius. Is it too late, I wonder, to back out now? And, faced with her first personal encounter with the high-school generation, Kate wanted to take to her heels and fly. At least my brothers know where they stand, she told herself grimly. You phony liberal, you.

She pulled herself together to greet the lady who attended the switchboard and kept a watchful eye on the large entrance hall.

"I'd like you to meet Miss Fansler," Anne was saying. "This is Miss Strikeland, who stands between us and the great outside world."

"How do you do," Kate said, to be interrupted by the switchboard.

"The Theban School," Miss Strikeland chirped; "certainly, just a moment please." She plunged in a plug with one hand, beckoning to Anne with the other. Anne moved in closer.

"He's here again," Miss Strikeland whispered.

"Who?"

"That man. Walking around over there. It's the second or third time he's come." Cautiously, Kate and Anne followed her glance, but the man had his profile to them and could be examined freely. He looked in his early seventies, impeccably dressed. He held his hat in his hand and gazed about him exactly as though he were in a museum he had come miles to visit. Certainly there wasn't much to gaze at—the occasional girl dashing through the lobby, the people who entered and came to Miss Strikeland's window for information, the members of the staff on their way to the staff lounge or one of the offices. Yet the elderly man seemed to study it all as though, as Ophelia said of Hamlet, he would draw it.

"How odd," Anne said. "He *looks* harmless enough. Have you asked him what he wants?"

"He says he just wants to look around. I pointed out that this was a school—after all, there isn't a sign outside and sometimes people don't know. He said he knew it was a school, the Theban School, and that's why he wanted to look around. He hoped I would be kind enough to allow him to do so. I told him he couldn't go upstairs, and he said he wouldn't. Last time he sat down on a bench and watched the girls leaving—he sat there for several hours."

"Miss Strikeland," Anne said, "do you suspect him of being a dirty old man?"

"Well, he doesn't look like it, does he? I've kept a pretty close eye on him. All the same, it's worrying."

"He's going," Kate said.

"So he is. Well," Anne said, "if he comes again, Miss Strikeland, you'd better let someone know. Miss Freund, for instance; she's good at this sort of problem."

"You're right," Miss Strikeland said. "Welcome to the Theban, Miss Fansler. Sorry to be so distracted."

"The same Miss Freund as in my day?" Kate asked. "Admissions, excuses, and frantic receiver of appeals for carfare?"

"The same. Except now she also handles bus passes, and is on very chummy terms with the local police precinct."

"Because of the boys in the gym?" Kate asked, following Anne back to the stairs.

"No. Because sometimes the girls no sooner poke their little noses outside the door than they are set on by gangs of kids—lower-class gangs, though it doesn't do to say so. But they taunt the Theban girls with being rich, so one rather gathers that's the point. After several hysterical parents' meetings, we now have a standard operating procedure. One of the girls returns immediately to the school and Miss Freund gets in touch with her policemen buddies. The girls are asked to report if they're molested on the buses or anywhere else. It's hard, really, to expect them to be simple and innocent in a world that's so criminal and brutal. Well," she added, pushing open a door and leading the way into a lunchroom where the din was so intense it struck one with palpable force, "How about lunch? I never know whether a tour like this sharpens the appetite or kills it. Good, I see Mrs. Banister. Shall we go and chat about dramatics at the Theban? Needless to say, we haven't even mentioned the problems of literature and seminars, except for the intrusion of that unfortunate poem. You aren't brooding, are you?"

"No more than is good for me."

"Splendid. Then sit down and introduce yourself, and I'll get you some lunch. It's either tuna-fish sandwich or chicken à la king. I recommend tuna fish."

Mrs. Banister proved to be a tiny woman of enormous vivacity and emphatic views which she enunciated with vigor and abandoned with alacrity and without regret if she was successfully challenged. She had an enormous affection for youngsters and respect for them—so much was immediately clear; certainly she herself appeared to have retained many of their better qualities. The gift of being able to establish rapport with young adults is rare enough; many people are good, or they think they are, with young children. Once past early childhood, however, the children often begin to find the nurses, kindergarten teachers, and baby lovers generally cloying and burdensome. Mrs. Banister was a rare specimen.

"I feel particularly giddy today," she told Kate, "because Andrew and I have finally solved the problem of New York transportation. Motorcycles. Last night we went to an evening thing complete with evening dress and I sat pillion behind Andrew. Marvelous. We had no trouble parking, and unlike the taxis we didn't have to wait hours with our meters ticking away even to approach the entrance. Benefit concert, Lincoln Center," she added, setting the scene.

"But suppose it rains?" Kate asked, greeting Anne and the tuna-fish sandwiches.

"Sou'westers, oilskin head to toe, and my evening slippers in a little plastic bag. One must move with the times or one is likely to get stuck in a traffic jam and never move at all. Not to mention pollution."

"Do you ride on a motorcycle to school?" Kate asked.

"No. Andrew, who has to get about much more, takes it during the day. I bicycle. Healthier, less pollution still, same sou'wester and plastic bag in case of rain. I hear the girls are looking forward to your seminar."

"Do you?" Kate said. "I wish I could say the same. The fact is, I've got a bad case of stage fright."

"Nonsense. Julia Stratemayer tells me you're frightfully good at your university. This is a bit more personal perhaps, but the twelves have one foot out the school door already. Quite grownup, really. I've got three of your *Antigone* bunch in one of my drama groups: Angelica Jablon, Betsy Stark, and Freemond Oliver."

"Is that actually her name?"

"Absolutely. I strongly suspect there was a Susan or something in front of the Freemond once upon a time, but it's plain Freemond Oliver as long as I've known her. She's quite extraordinary at Greek and Latin *and* athletics. Betsy Stark's quite another kettle of fish— devoted to every form of the comedy of manners from *The Way of the World* through Dorothy Sayers. She believes the great time in the theater after Shakespeare— and she insists, naturally, that *Much Ado About Nothing* is his greatest play—is the American comedy of the twenties and thirties, all sparkling confusions and wit with a wide streak of sentimentality up the middle. *The Philadelphia Story*, one gathers, is the prize of them all."

"My husband agrees with her. I'm surprised she wants to study the *Antigone*."

"Well, that may be just a little bit of my influence— not that you must think she's been persuaded against her inclinations, nothing of the sort. She's *very* fond of the *Odyssey* and considers the conversations between Odysseus and Athene the first witty man-woman exchanges in all literature. In fact, she says, there wasn't another such till Beatrice and Benedick, but no doubt she's exaggerating—the twelves do."

"And the third girl?" Kate asked, wondering how in the world she was going to conduct a seminar with an athletic Greek scholar and an admirer of George Kaufman's burdened with neither Greek nor humility.

"Angelica Jablon," Mrs. Banister said in a dreamy sort of way. "A *most* unusual girl, though less easily catalogued than the other two, at least in Theban terms. She, you see, is committed, *engagée* as the French say.

What excites her about the *Antigone* is that she feels it as the story of our times."

"Yikes. And no doubt she identifies with Antigone— I go to my death willingly for the right and all that sort of thing."

"Does that strike you as foolish?" Mrs. Banister said. "Perhaps I've misjudged . . ."

"Sorry," Kate said. "I'm afraid I tend to come all over scholarly at the wrong moments. I've learned, you see, to be wary of the student who finds some work which alone holds the secret of life. On the other hand, such a student, if she has real devotion to scholarship, may make such a discovery the start of some real work. I'm sure that will be the case with Angelica."

"Perhaps. No doubt you will find all the girls stimulating; I'm certain at least that you'll keep them within hailing distance of the scholarly approach, which is beyond me—that's why I direct drama groups and don't teach anything. A matter of temperament."

Kate wanted to ask if any of the girls was given to the writing of rhymed doggerel—Ogden Nash had a lot to answer for, Kate often thought, having invented a form of verse which no one but he seemed able to grasp the first thing about—but she felt a mysterious reluctance to mention the seminar poster. If I can't straighten it out alone with them, she thought, I better quit now.

"Hi." Julia Stratemayer stood balancing a tray at Kate's arm. "May I join you or are you enmeshed in Greek drama?"

"Good to see you," Kate said.

"I've been following you and Anne around the building like a blasted bloodhound, but you always seemed to have just left wherever I was. Miss Strikeland told me you'd probably alighted here."

"Did she mention her mysterious visitor?"

"She did. I'm afraid she's getting the wind up a bit, though from what I can gather he couldn't look more harmless or benign. Still, one can't have men, however ancient, loitering around school buildings, so when he appears again, Miss Freund is going to go down and cross-examine. Why is the tuna fish one gets in boughten sandwiches always so *wet?*"

Kate settled back more comfortably in Julia's presence. She would have liked a cigarette, but of course one could not smoke in the school dining room— another of the disadvantages of teaching at the Theban was borne in upon her.

"We can smoke later in the staff cloakroom, if you are about to suffer from nicotine withdrawal symptoms," Julia said, reading her mind. They were in fact close friends, though they had never cared for each other all through their years as classmates at the Theban. Was there a moral here somewhere about childhood friendships, Kate wondered. Those who had been her closest friends through school, even in the last years, were now acquaintances whom she encountered infrequently, though gladly enough. Julia, when young, had seemed interested in little but volleyball and the domestic virtues; she had not only entered, in her senior year, some nationwide homemaker contest, she had actually won it, which seemed to Kate the absolute end. Julia, in her turn, considered Kate overintellectual, which she was, and snobbish, which she wasn't. Because Kate had had, since her fourteenth year, a long, lean model's figure, natural taste in clothes, and the money to dress with stunning simplicity, she had impressed a lot of people as more "proper," more devoted to correctness, than she was, which in fact was not at all. She and Julia after graduation had gone their different, predictable ways, Kate to graduate school and a series of mad jobs ("If I ever publish a book," Kate used to say, "I want to be able to say on the jacket that, like Arthur Koestler, I have worked at everything and sold lemonade in the streets of Haifa." Kate had never been to Haifa, with or without lemonade, but the phrase always stood to her for the ultimate in worldly experience). Julia had quit college at the end of her sophomore year, to marry, move to the suburbs, and bring up a large family. Hers, rather than Kate's, was the typical pattern of their generation. But Julia, when everyone least expected it, had proved to be untypical. She had made up her mind quite suddenly one day never to set foot in a country club again. Her husband, it transpired after the first real conversation they had had in fifteen years, was delighted with the thought of moving back to the city, with its public transportation for the children and its noncommuting for him. She had finished college, taken her master's degree in literature, and turned up looking for work at the Theban.

Miss Tyringham had nothing for her, and in any case took on Theban alumnae only if they had had experience elsewhere, but she heard of a need for a substitute teacher in another school and steered Julia into that. Five years later, Julia was a member of the English Department at the Theban, and six years later she was in charge of curriculum revision. She turned out to possess exactly the right qualifications for this odd job, having a highly organized mind, a flexible attitude toward change, and the amazing ability to talk about the problems of curriculum with parents' groups. She assured them that, while the Theban was undertaking many fundamental changes, nothing fundamental about the Theban would be changed. Obviously, a prize. Kate had run into her shortly after her move from the suburbs, stopped to talk, and discovered a friend for life.

"Miss Tyringham's pleased," Julia said as they walked toward the faculty lounge for the promised smoke. "She hated the thought of fobbing off someone from inside who hadn't really prepared the seminar— it would rather have taken the bloom off the whole thing."

"The bloom," Kate said, "will come off me instead. Frankly, I'm having qualms. Look, Julia, ought this damn thing to be a bull session or a structural study? I mean, should we sit around and rap about sex and women's lib and the Black Panthers, should we really do a solid piece of work on the *Antigone*, or do we alternate—as though that were possible?"

"Start sounding very structured, of course. One's first session is always plans, schedules, assignments, and expectations. Though you may not believe it, the girls will be to some extent scared of you from the great big university world. If, eventually, Haemon's stabbing himself and dying while embracing the dead Antigone leads to a discussion of sex, discuss away. I guess what I'm saying is, ride easy with it. If you start feeling the onset of hysteria, which I don't for a moment imagine you will, press the panic button and I'll come and force brandy down your throat."

"When," Kate asked, "did your conversation become so replete with slogany phrases—an academic habit, I take it?"

"Since talking to parents. Believe me, Kate, the girls are nothing to it. I'll trade you the ninth-grade mothers for the *Antigone* any day."

Four

KATE met Reed for dinner at the Plaza; he took one look at her, ordered martinis, and politely inquired about her day.

"Oh, the hell with it," Kate said. "What about the draft?"

"Would I have married you, I wonder, if I had really considered the ramifications of all your nephews? If the war goes on long enough we will no doubt have to go through all this with Jack's little brothers."

"Did the draft turn out to be so complicated, even now that they've got a lottery?"

"Especially now that they've got a lottery. Never mind that for the moment. Tell me about the Theban."

"Well, there's nothing really to tell till I meet the class on Monday, but I already know it contains three girls from whom I could see trouble coming if I were blindfolded in the middle of a foggy night with no moon."

"It's always been the problem, you know, in dealing with adolescents, as Terence Rattigan pointed out. They're too old to spank and too young to hit over the jaw, if anybody ever thought of doing either these days, which of course they don't."

"You'll be overjoyed to hear that one of the darlings is an admirer of comedies in your period, as we say in graduate school. She thinks literature leaps more or less from Shakespeare to *The Philadelphia Story*, omitting, of course, most of the masterpieces of the last three hundred years."

"Ah, the martinis—things will soon look brighter. Cheer up, perhaps she'll talk like a Philip Barry character."

"I don't know what she talks like," Kate said taking a sip and lighting a cigarette, "because I haven't met her. I must say I would prefer the Plaza to the Theban dining room even if I couldn't smoke or drink here— imagine what it must be like to teach in a girls' boarding school. Well, let's not imagine and rattle our nerves further. I learned about the three students from Mrs. Banister, who does dramatics—not as a class but as an activity, and obviously she takes the label 'activity' with appalling seriousness. She encouraged the three girls to take my seminar; it's not clear whether I'm to be grateful or to poison her chicken à la king, but the latter I rather fancy, since her dramatics bit consists in everyone being emotional off the top of her head, which is definitely *not* my scene."

"Sounds like the encounter sort of business."

"It does, and I gather is, at least part of the time. That

is, sometimes the girls write plays and act them out, sometimes they act out their longings and emotions, and sometimes they play guessing games to stimulate their imaginations, which need stimulation as much as I need this job, which is not at all."

"Guessing games? Charades?"

"Not exactly. Julia explained it all to me while holding my hand during today's earlier collapse. For example, I say to you: 'A man comes out of a restaurant where he has just tasted albatross. He kills himself. Who is he and why does he kill himself?' You ask all sorts of intelligent and searching questions and eventually discover. Want to know the answer?"

"Well, after a second martini I don't mind if you tell me, provided it isn't so long they'll throw us out to the bar and refuse to let us order dinner."

"No more than two sentences—and never mind the remark about the length of my sentences. I will be brief, as Polonius said to Gertrude before going on forever. You know, I'm beginning to have more and more sympathy for Polonius, whose only trouble was that he was operating in one world by the rules of another."

"The man has just tasted albatross," Reed said, tasting his second martini.

"Yes. Well, after all sorts of questions it drearily transpires that he is a sailor, has been shipwrecked, only three men left, they had nothing to eat but albatross and a mate recently beheaded by a falling mast; to save everyone's feelings the cook mixed the two up so that they wouldn't have to know which they were eating. Now, having tasted albatross, the sailor knows what he ate was human flesh and he kills himself at the horror of the thing."

"Why on earth?"

"Why on earth what?"

"Well, I meant why on earth kill himself at the horror of the thing, but now that you ask, why bother with the whole bit? Why not just act *Hamlet* or *Design for Living?*" Reed caught the headwaiter's eye. "We'll order now," he said. "What will you have?" he asked Kate.

"Hemlock and sour cream."

"Oh, Kate, do pull yourself together. Why panic over a bunch of kids?"

"They wrote me a nasty poem and put it on the wall—it was a threat, actually."

"Did it rhyme?"

"More or less. I'd rather it hadn't."

"Tell them so and set them each to writing you a poem about Antigone. That'll be one in the eye for them!"

"Reed," Kate said, "you're a genius."

"Only on certain Thursdays in February," Reed said. "Have some pâté, cheer up, and I'll tell you how to avoid the draft."

They were well into the main course, and halfway through their bottle of wine before Kate persuaded Reed to return to the draft. "I thought," she said, "that the point of the lottery was to end all the unfair exemptions, like being in college or graduate school or being a father, though I've always privately thought that fatherhood ought to be allowed as an exemption provided the father stayed home all day with the little one. From what I hear, he'd enlist so fast they wouldn't have to bother with a draft."

"Not a bad idea at that," Reed said. "Well, the lottery, like so many cures, is worse than the disease, only in different ways. Disease, in fact, is the operative word. Almost seventy percent of the men are found to be 4F at their first physical, and thirty percent of the rest are let off on physical grounds the next time around."

"They all have flat feet, you mean?"

"Or just about anything else you can name, including braces on their teeth or hair that has to be shampooed every day."

"Tell me another."

"With pleasure. The army considerately publishes a guide to what it considers physical fitness, and anyone can buy it from the Government Printing Office. The country is now full of draft counseling agencies, as they call themselves, though not as full as New York is, and each of them has a well-thumbed copy. Anyway, the induction centers are so understaffed that they have to rely on the word of the would-be-draftee's doctor, and most doctors are sympathetic to the poor kids. The army in its proud old days didn't want anyone who was very ugly, wet his bed, acted queer or was, or bit his nails. Now they're no doubt rueing the day, but the simple fact is almost everyone around New York manages to get off for *something*.

"If," Reed went on, filling his wine glass and Kate's, "they don't get a physical exemption, they can claim to be a conscientious objector. There are various ways of diddling around with one's status, gambling on one's lottery number, or, if all else fails, simply failing to show up for induction."

"Don't they find you and put you in jail?"

"In theory. In practice, after the hideously understaffed Selective Service unit has written around to make sure the guy actually did get the letter, a year has passed, and then they simply can't follow up all the cases. Not one man in the city has so far been indicted for delinquency, as a matter of fact. *And* if the worst should happen and the guy who failed to show up for induction was found, tried, and convicted, he would end up serving considerably less than a year in one of the better prisons. He would have to serve with the army in Vietnam for two years."

"Has it always been like that, with only innocents like me remembering everyone but cowards and operators marching off to war, with the cross of Jesus going on before? My mind does seem to run to hymns lately, the effect of the Theban no doubt. All the guys I knew . . ."

"That, my love, was a war the country was behind. There have always been operators who got out of active service and there always will be, but, though I haven't looked into the history of the thing, I have the impression that this situation developed because of the great unpopularity of this war, which is even more unpopular in New York than elsewhere, as our Vice President keeps telling us. And don't think I've covered all the ways of not getting drafted, because I've hardly begun."

"In that case, what is the problem with Jack? Can't he have braces put on his teeth? Anyway, he's got asthma; he told us so."

"But he is young and full of principles for which he is willing to suffer, always so embarrassing an attitude, though I *think* I have persuaded him to suffer at Harvard. The point is, if he registers as a C.O., which is what he wants to do, he will be involved in litigation, which is long, expensive, and unlikely to be paid for by his rich papa, though according to Jack's lights that is the only honorable course to follow. The question must ultimately be faced, I think, as to whether a draftee has the right to distinguish between wars—a sticky point if there ever was one. In my opinion, if you don't mind my saying so, I think your brother is handling this in the worst possible way. But at least he's standing by the truth as he sees it, you've got to give him that, and so is his son. I'd be likelier to help the kid slip through the net while agreeing with him that he was right in principle—but I always was unfortunately given to the comfortable way of doing things."

"Nonsense. You'd never have married me if you were. I understand why the Theban is on the spot—why all schools are. The students want them to be in the vanguard of social progress, and the parents and faculty see it as their duty to defend the rearguard. A hell of a choice, and I see the students' point, but as Dorothy Sayers mentioned somewhere, all epic actions are fought in the rearguard, at Roncevaux and Thermopylae."

"Writers prefer rearguard battles—the issues are clear and tragic. In life, however, I suspect the important actions, though they will never make an epic, are fought in the beginning, before anybody knows what the battle's all about."

"No doubt you're right, damn it. If I like the battles which are epic, what is rearguard me doing in a seminar room with the vanguard young? Answer me that."

"What you need," Reed said, "is to go home to bed."

"Not so soon after dinner, as the lady said in *Private*

Lives," Kate responded, looking pleased with herself for the first time that evening.

Monday morning found Kate, with the calm the professional always finds in his own arena, however anxious he may have been before, seated at the head of the table in the seminar room with the students seated on each side—like a king dining with the regiment, Kate thought. The challenging verse was gone from the wall.

"What," Kate asked, as an opening remark, "has become of the poem on the wall?" This, while certainly plunging *in medias res*, as the ancients recommended, left something to be desired as a conversation opener.

The girls looked at one another, not turning their heads but shifting their eyes back and forth in a most disconcerting way. "We had hoped," one of the girls said—she was clearly used to speaking for the group when a spokesman was required—"that you had not seen it. It was thought better of and removed."

"And your name?" Kate asked. "We might as well get that established. I'll read the list of names given to me, and you each claim your own. O.K.?"

"I'm Freemond Oliver," the girl who had spoken said.

"Ah," Kate said, in what she trusted were sepulchral tones. "Angelica Jablon?"

"Here." The girl who spoke had an expressive face and heavy, curly hair. She looked outspoken, unhappy, unsure of herself and, Kate was pleased to notice, kind. *Engagé* fighters for the right—that is, for the left— were often, in Kate's experience, remarkably brutal.

"Irene Rexton."

"Here." A remarkably pretty girl, demure in appearance, with a face so lovely and appealing that one decided, immediately and quite unfairly, that she was probably brainless. Her long blond hair fell over her face and she languidly pushed it back behind her ears with a gesture more seductive than she could possibly have realized. So, at least, Kate hoped.

"Betsy Stark." Ah, thought Kate, the comedy-of-manners child. Now why should I have expected her to look like Katharine Hepburn?—an association of ideas, no doubt. It was, perhaps, an association that had occurred to Betsy Stark, who was a most unpretty girl, but of the sort who does not try to improve her natural endowments with a too lavish application of the current fads in makeup or hair style. Whatever her commitment to wit, she had decided to try to accept herself as she was, which Kate thought interesting. She was the only girl in the room whose face was innocent of eye makeup; in my day, Kate thought, it would have been lipstick. Also in my day, she realized looking around, we always wore the uniforms. These girls wore different-color shirts with pants or odd skirts. I refuse to think about the question of uniforms, Kate thought, deciding that the reasons for not teaching in the school you have yourself attended are numerous, though hidden.

"Elizabeth McCarthy. I understand," Kate added, "that you're new to the Theban this year, having transferred from the Sacred Heart in Detroit. Did you know that when you transferred to the Theban you would get seminars?"

"She came because she's what my little brother calls a Roaming Catholic," Betsy Stark said.

Elizabeth McCarthy smiled at this sally. "I've always been with the Mesdames," she said, "and when we moved to New York I thought I'd like to switch. I've had seven years of Latin, but no Greek."

"Let's be quite clear about the whole question of Greek," Kate said. "The last Greek I had was in this very building a long time ago, so I will be glad to learn from those of you who know Greek, and happy to share my ignorance with those of you who don't. And you," Kate added, turning to the last girl, "must be Alice Kirkland."

"If I must I must," the girl said. Kate raised her eyebrows, but decided to let that one pass. "Ride easy with it," Julia had advised, and Kate was prepared to follow this counsel up to a point. She was, as always, astonished to discover how sharply she reacted to rudeness.

"That takes care of that," Kate said. "Now, to return to the verse which appeared and disappeared, in each case so provocatively, from the wall. It is perfectly true that I might never have seen it had I not been given a tour of the school, and it is equally true that discretion might perhaps suggest the pretense that I had not seen it. But—I saw it, and if there is one rule I have learned from the young, it is that pretense is to be avoided at all costs. We might even say there is some connection with the *Antigone* there, but let that pass. The verse was a challenge to which I intend to respond. I suggest that each of you write a poem derived from the *Antigone*, perhaps from some minor point in it. You will be able to sharpen your versifying techniques, and I will feel better.

"Now, I'll pass around a reading list of works which seem to me to come to grips in an interesting way with some of the problems of the *Antigone*. As we go along, you may discover other works equally or more interesting, and we will add them. I'd like to suggest as a procedure that, since there are seven of us and fourteen weeks, we each take charge of assigning the reading and directing the discussion in two seminar meetings. I'll start next week, you six will follow in succeeding meetings, and then we'll go round again. Any comments, suggestions, or spontaneous versifying?"

"I can't write poetry," Alice Kirkland said. "I never could. There are seminars in verse writing, but I didn't choose to take them."

"Well," Kate said, "I'm sure it's not too late to choose your way out of this one. Just go in and see Miss Tyringham or her assistant. If you stay, write a poem for next time. It needn't be a good poem, you know; it can be silly stuff or, which is always good practice, an Italian sonnet, a villanelle, or a sestina. If you have a strict form to stay within, you at least have fun even if you don't come up with one of the world's great lyrics."

Alice Kirkland opened her mouth to argue and then, as five pairs of eyes bore into hers, ceased. It was clear that Alice would go on playing the devil's advocate only so long as the others were behind her—something which it was well worth six bad verses to have discovered.

"I've thought of a few possible topics for discussion. We don't have to do them, but they're fairly obvious and likely to come up in one form or another anyway. Perhaps they'll set you to thinking about what aspects of the play really interest you. Incidentally, though I do tend to go on rather—it's a habit which, like smoking,

I seem unable or unwilling to abandon—do interrupt me at any time.

"I've only just begun reading about the *Antigone*, and I want to be perfectly frank in telling you that. I do not expect to remain one lesson ahead of the class, as is the usual desperate remedy of pedagogues. I expect you'll catch up with me or overtake me, and my only wish is that we shall all leave the course knowing more about the *Antigone* and perhaps about how to approach a living, vital work than we did before."

"I don't understand," Elizabeth McCarthy said. "Is the *Antigone* any more living or vital than Caesar, or Cicero, say, and does it have to be approached differently?"

"I think the *Antigone* is more living, but the point is arguable and, as I have said, I hope you will argue it. There are, after all, two kinds of literature, broadly speaking: that which still speaks to us and our particular anguishes of today, and that which spoke to its contemporary audience and can only have a scholarly interest for us as we try to discover what the work meant to those for whom it was written. Take a play like, oh, *Bartholomew Fair* by Ben Jonson. It's a wonderful comedy if you've got up enough about the sixteenth century to be able to get the jokes. Shakespeare, on the other hand, speaks, as we say, to our condition. The study of Jonson's play I would like to call a task in literary history, the study of Shakespeare's a task in literary criticism, but it happens that is not a very safe distinction to make, and I hope you will all be quite clear that I am not making it." The class grinned and Kate felt better.

"Our interest," Freemond Oliver said, "even for

those of us who struggled through the play in Greek, is that it's so very *now*—I mean, the story of a tyrant who wants to impose his rules and his ideas of patriotism, and this young woman, this single individual, who insists on following her own conscience about what is right, and who wants to act from love."

"Sure," Kate said, "but I would argue with you whether Creon is a tyrant—there *is* a good deal of right on his side, which also makes the play so modern. You can say if you want, and George Eliot has, that the conflict is between individual judgment and the conventions of society, but it is dangerous to assume that the conventions of society are, despite our sneering use of the word 'conventional,' necessarily wrong. Without some conventions, each day would be a new battle back at the beginning of time."

"Anyone who says he will stone to death whoever disobeys his rules is a tyrant," Angelica Jablon proclaimed.

"Creon has a lot of right on his side," Betsy Stark said, "particularly if you give him credit for changing his mind, which seems to be the human accomplishment least often accomplished. Imagine Bill Buckley changing his mind about student movements or Eleanor Roosevelt."

"It's like the arguments over closing the school for Moratorium Day," Irene Rexton said. "We ended up having a so-called compromise; that is, we came to school and had discussion groups on the Vietnam War. But that didn't leave me, for example, if I believed that the war was an honorable one, able to attend school in the ordinary way, which surely I had a right to do."

"Isn't it 'school' discussing a war the country's all

hung up on over?" Angelica asked, with more heat and prepositions than were perhaps desirable.

"The question of whether or not Creon is a tyrant is therefore on the agenda," Kate quietly said, "as is the connected question of whether Creon or Antigone is in fact the 'hero' of Sophocles' play. Expert opinion, as is its unpleasant habit, is divided. We do know that the role of Antigone was played by the first actor, and that of Creon by the third, which is an example of how historical knowledge can cast light. And then, Antigone dies halfway through the play, never having doubted her destiny, while Creon is alone at the end of the play living out his terrible fate and managing, as Betsy pointed out, to change his mind, alas, too late.

"Now just a moment," Kate said, holding up her hand, as several of the girls tried to speak. "I told you to interrupt me and now I won't let you, so typical of aging teachers, I know. But if I can just get the list of possible subjects completed, I promise you, I solemnly swear, that starting with the next session I will allow you to interrupt me, I may even shut up altogether once in a while. We must get the semester's schedule made out today so as to have all the mechanics done with once and for all. Creon as tyrant or hero is one subject; I would like to suggest . . ."

"Will you put your money where your mouth is?" Alice Kirkland asked. The five pairs of eyes again revolved toward Alice Kirkland, this time returning to observe Kate's face.

"If you can manage to rephrase that question so that it exudes some slight air of courtesy, I shall consider it." Kate allowed the silence which followed this statement to remain unbroken.

"What I meant," Alice Kirkland said finally, "is that maybe you would want to agree to put some sum of money, you know, a dime or something, into a pot every time you talk for more than three minutes at a stretch and then, the end of the year, we can have a bash."

"Three minutes it is," Kate answered, "if you'll allow me, in addition, five minutes at the beginning and end for setting forth and summing up. After all, I'm responsible if we all fall flat on our faces. What's more I'll double whatever the amount is at the end, enough to make it a feast. Will you keep track of the dimes, Elizabeth?"

"All right, but I think the suggestion is rude, presumptuous and just plain nasty. Why take the seminar if she doesn't want to hear you talk?"

"There," Kate said, "I think you're being unfair. She wants to try out her ideas, which she can't do if she's forever listening to mine. Since, however, it's I who am being presumptuous and just plain nasty today, let me go on with a list of possible topics for reports and discussions. Has anyone any brilliant suggestions?"

"Why did she have to bury her brother at all?" Irene Rexton asked. "It had been forbidden, he *was* a traitor to his country, and anyway, what did she accomplish by throwing some dust over his rotten old corpse?"

"Oh, God, let's not go into *that*!" Freemond Oliver said. "Burial to the Greeks meant something different than it means to us, and that's it. You didn't leave the dead to rot, that was divine law, and obviously it was important or Creon wouldn't have bothered about not burying the body in the first place. The facts are right in the play and, anyhow, it's a tired subject and tiresome besides."

57

Kate wished, for the first in what was to be a very long series of such wishes, that the young would not be quite so cruel to one another. "That question has rather died from view, I think," she said to Irene Rexton, "though it was very much argued about at one time. Another question which might interest you is less hashed over: How original was Sophocles in his presentation of the Antigone story? He's credited with originating Haemon as Antigone's betrothed; Ismene, her sister, as a foil to Antigone; and the idea of putting Tiresias into the play. Would an account of what Euripides is thought to have done with the story in his lost play on Antigone or what Aeschylus did with it in his *Seven Against Thebes* interest you?"

"I'd like to study what Anouilh did with the story," Betsy Stark said. "Personally, I think Anouilh stinks on ice, but it's interesting that he wrote such a play, that he left Tiresias out, and that the Nazis let him put it on in Paris. That ties in with the bit about Is Creon a tyrant or isn't he, tune in next week and find out same time same station, because supposedly the Nazis let him put on that play because they thought Creon was right, and Antigone, who represented the French, was wrong."

"The Free French," Kate rather breathlessly said, "as opposed to the French government which had made a pact with Hitler." She had long accustomed herself to the fact that such events, to her the very cornerstone of contemporary history, were just ancient history, and rather shopworn at that, to students who had not been born until twelve years or more after the fall of France. "A good idea," she said to Betsy. "What has always struck me so forcibly about the *Antigone* is the way it sort of floats into the Greek theater—the whole story of Antigone's burying her brother contrary to Creon's edict isn't even part of the tradition—and then disappears until the nineteenth century. Then it's discovered by a woman writer, George Eliot, as central to her ideas about identity and destiny."

"It's the sort of story that would have to wait around for a woman to pick it up," Angelica Jablon said. "Antigone had to be a woman; it's why Creon can keep sneering at her. 'No woman's going to tell me what to do,' and that sort of thing. Only a woman was enough of a slave to like require the kind of guts Antigone had."

"So Virginia Woolf suggests, more or less," Kate said. "Would that be a topic for you?"

"I don't mind if that's what you want," Angelica said, "but it seems to me it's really a story of individuals against the Establishment, the military-industrial complex like, and all that."

"I'll do the woman bit," Alice Kirkland said. "How about comparing it to *Lysistrata?*"

"No harm comparing it to anything you want," Kate said, "if you think the comparison isn't just superficial."

"It's not even a comparison," Betsy said. "One is a real modern problem, the other's the same old comic turn—woman's only weapon is sex, so she uses it."

"I agree," Angelica said. "Antigone stands for humanity against arbitrary state law. That she's a woman just makes it harder to stand up to Creon. But she doesn't use her sex to bury her brother."

"She uses her sex, or rather, her sex matters in her having Haemon on her side," Elizabeth said.

"If Haemon were really a male chauvinist like

Creon," Betsy said, "he would have gone for Ismene who's much more 'feminine,' if you'll excuse the expression."

"Perhaps," Kate said, "we might discuss the role of Tiresias in that connection."

"He's certainly one of the few—perhaps the only true—androgynous characters there are," Betsy added.

"What I like about talking to you," Alice Kirkland said, "is that it's so *educative*."

"The fact is, I wonder why someone doesn't write a comedy of manners about *him*," Betsy said. "Not to mention the boy he is always leaning on—in play after play, he never gets a chance to open his little mouth, like the bat boy with a baseball team."

"So tell us what's 'androgynous' already," Angelica said.

"There goes Angelica, the Jewish mother—cut it out, Angie," Freemond Oliver said. "Angie wrote a skit for the drama group about Saint Mary and Saint Elizabeth as Jewish mothers. It was pretty funny, I'll admit, but let's not make it a habit, O.K., Angie?" Her eyes, like Kate's, were on Elizabeth, who looked embarrassed.

"O.K., Oliver, so what's—how do you define 'androgynous'?"

"Both men and women," Betsy said, "have aspects of both sexes, with one sex predominating if you're lucky, and one sex predominating too much if you're unlucky enough to end up with a sewing circle or the Elks. Shaw called *them* manly men and womanly women, but we'll let that one go by. Tiresias had actually been both a man and a woman, so was the only person who could report on what it was like to be both sexes, an enviable position, was it not?" My God, Kate thought, she's got a chance to be something, if she doesn't try too hard and burn it out. Another reason for not teaching the really young—you see so much promise and most of it gone before they get their wisdom teeth.

"Well," Betsy continued, "Hera and Zeus got into a rap one day about who had a better time making out; Zeus said women did, and Hera said men did, and so of course they decided to ask old Tiresias, who'd been there and knew." She paused dramatically, having reached the high point of her story.

"Sooo?" Elizabeth asked, making them all laugh.

"So Tiresias said women did, and Hera was so mad she made him blind. Zeus couldn't undo that, since one god can't ever undo another's work, but he tried to make it up to Tiresias by giving him the gift of prophecy, which has always seemed to me pretty poor compensation, since he keeps coming on in play after play, led by that boy, and getting yelled at by all the major characters. Of course," she concluded, "he has the satisfaction of always being right."

"Thank you, Betsy," Kate said, recognizing a curtain line when she heard one. "If anyone doesn't have a topic, stop by and discuss it for a minute. Next time I'll distribute the schedule and you distribute the poems. Each of you get your poem dittoed so we can each have a copy."

"Jesus, I don't want anyone else to look at it," Alice Kirkland said.

Kate bravely refrained from advising her to put her money where her mouth was. "The point of a seminar," she said in her best pedagogical tones, "is so that we may all discuss everything together, and learn not to get our vanity involved. Impossible, but our reach must exceed our grasp or what are seminars for?" And she rapidly adjourned this one, before anybody could decide to try to answer *that* question.

Five

FEBRUARY, with its alternating freezes and false promises of spring, gave way to March which, though it promised more, was less readily believed. People went around reminding each other that the blizzard of '88 had been in March and mid-March at that. Mrs. Johnson, still at home in traction and frantic for diversion, was glad to hear Kate's reports on the *Antigone* seminar.

"Are you using the Jebb translation after all?" she asked Kate, who had come to visit and report.

"Yes, though they've read through at least three others, for comparison, and we spend some time discussing them. It's odd really that I should prefer Jebb, who's full of thees and thous, verbs with unfamiliar endings and inverted sentences—everybody talks the way one might have supposed Englishmen would have talked at the time of the *Antigone* if there had been an

English language, though of course one knows they would have talked Anglo-Saxon or something if there had been—I'm not making this at all clear."

"I understand exactly what you mean," Mrs. Johnson said, laughing and then grimacing. "Oh, dear," she added, "it's exactly like Saint Sebastian when they asked *him* if it hurt and he said only when I laugh—coughing and sneezing hurt worse, of course, but I don't mind *not* coughing and sneezing. The most recent translations—Watling and Wyckoff and Townsend and so forth—would certainly be easier for actors, and I suppose manage to turn the speeches into idiomatic English, not to say hep talk—but I too prefer Jebb. Can it be that we resent Antigone sounding as up to date as all that?"

"Well, when you decided the *Antigone* would be relevant, you certainly had your finger on the pulse of the times, to coin a phrase. The girls have got so involved they're not only doing twice as much work as I would have dreamed of requiring, but three of them are in Mrs. Banister's drama group, and they've been improvising on *Antigone* for weeks now, so she tells me. How these dead bones do take on flesh given half a chance."

"I'm sure a great part of the credit is yours," Mrs. Johnson loyally said. "It's why I insisted they couldn't just shove a classicist into the spot—not that there aren't classicists who could have done it, heaven knows, but the ones at the Theban are quite properly interested in the structure of the language and the historical background to Greek lives."

"I won't argue the point," Kate said, "because I've discovered that my modesty is almost always taken for disingenuousness, when the truth of the matter is, as Churchill said of Attlee, I've got a lot to be modest about. We've had, actually, only one contretemps in the seminar, at the very beginning—I won't go into it now, because it's an awfully silly story, really—but the upshot was I insisted on each of the girls writing a poem about the *Antigone,* taking off from some minor point, you know, nothing crashingly profound or full of oxymorons, just a verse. I thought I'd leave them with you, to cheer your hours lying here trussed up like a steer."

"Considering you've brought me flowers and the life of Lytton Strachey, I don't think you need to feel any more responsibility for my dragging hours, but thank you all the same for the kind thought." She began to look through the poems, just glancing at them in anticipation of reading them later, but she stopped at one and read it through.

"Now I rather like this," she said, "though I'd be hard put to tell you why. She didn't even rhyme, as Horatio complained to Hamlet."

Kate looked over the edge of the bed. "Oh, yes," she said, "that's Betsy's. I too am rather fond of it; she's got a gift for ideas, but she's got to learn to take the time to find the exact words and put them in the proper order. Perhaps she ought to consider writing in Latin, where the order doesn't really matter." She read the poem again over Mrs. Johnson's shoulder.

You remember, in the Greek plays, Tiresias
Had a boy who led him on stage and off,
Through all his calls to prophecy, standing
Through all the stated visions, waiting to move
Out of the range of Oepidus' or Creon's anger?

What I want to know—where is that boy?
Did he one day say to Tiresias,
"I am grown and can no longer lead you"?
I suspect he grew up, became manly,
Taller perhaps than Tiresias, more erect and,
Seeking manhood, or what he took for
  manhood,
Left the presence of prophetic, androgynous
  wisdom.
Or did he, leading such blind truth,
Remain Tiresias'—as the stage directions say,
His boy?

"Trust Betsy to write about a character who only had a walk-on," Mrs. Johnson said. "Well, I have high hopes of Betsy, though she's not really at home among the tragic Greeks. She would have appreciated Lytton Strachey," she added, resting her hand on the volumes Kate had brought.

"I will leave you to him," Kate said. "Try to cheer up by thinking of all the reports you won't have to write—the worst part of school teaching."

"In exchange for doing *something* this very minute, taking a walk or playing hopscotch, I would gladly write every report in the school."

"I know—as Carlyle said to Geraldine Jewsbury under somewhat different circumstances, these are sorry times for a young woman of genius." Kate said her goodbyes to Mrs. Johnson, who was reaching for the small sheaf of poems.

"The poor thing is bored to death," Kate reported to Reed that evening. "She would so much rather be doing the seminar than lying there, even without any dreary orthopedic problems, while I, such are the ironies of life, would love to have nothing to do but lie on my back and do the work I'm supposed to be doing anyway. Well, the happy man has learned to use what the gods give—I don't remember who said that. but it was a classical author; I seem to be thinking in classical authors these days. At least if the Theban takes more time than I had anticipated, it no longer takes all my time and energy. I've learned to cope with the girls in the seminar, to follow the discussions into the waywardest of bypaths, and leave all the problems of the younger generations to older and wiser heads—well, wiser anyway. By the time March has assumed its lamblike demeanor, I expect to have got the Theban comfortably in proportion—or does that sound like hubris, which always gets the gods into such a pet?"

"Kate dear," Reed said, "I do wish you would assure me once and for all that you don't really believe in the Greek gods. You know, Olympus has turned into a housing development, and they've got a Hilton Hotel in the middle of the Elysian Fields."

"Hush," Kate said. "They'll hear you."

Kate and Reed had just finished the dinner dishes, turned off the kitchen light, and nearly wound up their nightly discussion of whether or not a household of two people really had use for an electric dishwasher, when the telephone rang.

"What a household of two people definitely hasn't use for is a telephone," Reed said peevishly.

Kate answered in the hall.

"Ah," came Miss Tyringham's voice, "thank heaven I've found you at home. Could you possibly, out of the kindness of your heart, pop over here a moment; the school building, that is? I can't take any more time to explain now, but our gratitude will be boundless. I know, I know, you're thinking I've said that before and it already is, but—please, Kate. Angelica's asking for you, among others."

"Angelica!"

"Say you'll hop in a taxi right now."

"All right, I'll be there." Kate hung up the phone. "Damn and blast! Athene heard you, if not Zeus himself. They've got a crisis," she added, somewhat incoherently.

"Goody," Reed said. "It'll give me a chance to get our stuff together for the income tax. A blessing in disguise. I'd never get it done if you were here to talk to."

"If there's one thing I can't *stand*," Kate said, scrambling into her coat, "it's people who look on the *bright* side."

The school building, when Kate got out of the taxi, looked dark and empty—for one horrible moment she wondered if she could have imagined the phone call or, worse, if someone had enticed her to this deserted street for God knew what sinister reasons. Her pulse had begun to race, which annoyed her further, when the door opened and Julia Stratemayer beckoned from within the dark hall. "Thank heaven," Kate said. "I was beginning to imagine all sorts of eerie things."

"Imagine away," Julia gloomily said. "You wouldn't be able to imagine this mess if you thought with both hands for a fortnight."

"How cheerful. No bodies, I hope. I more or less promised Reed to give up bodies when I married him."

"Not a *dead* body," Julia ominously said. "We can't stay here whispering. There's a conference in Miss Tyringham's office. Come on."

Kate was glad of Julia's companionship as they walked through the halls. She had never really thought of the building as dark before and began to admire the sheer guts of the boys who had broken in to use the gym and mutilate its floor. The school building was often open at night, of course, for parents' meetings, dances, plays, concerts, but then the lobby, stairs, and elevators were lit in the ordinary way so that the whole place looked quite as usual, though without the children screaming up and down the halls.

"Lucky you weren't having a parents' meeting when whatever happened happened," Kate said, more to hear her own, or any, voice, than because it seemed to her a particularly pertinent remark.

"If there had been a parents' meeting this wouldn't have happened. It had to be a night when the building was closed, you see."

"Oh," Kate said, who didn't see but supposed she soon would. "Why do you have parents' meetings at night?" she asked. "I thought the mothers always came in the afternoon and were fed tea and well-bred cookies afterward, to revive them."

"We've been doing this for years now," Julia said, "in the happy thought that fathers want to attend too and are, of course, far too busy with the important things of the world to spare afternoon hours." Julia's voice trailed off as they reached Miss Tyringham's office.

"Simply let it ring," Miss Tyringham was saying. "Just plug my line, though, in case I have to make a call. You might know," she added to Julia, "that someone would see the ambulance and call to inquire what the crisis was, if any. I've always been most pleased with the way the Theban mothers keep in touch with us if they've got the slightest worry, but tonight I could have done without any curiosity. The school is supposed to be closed at this hour, and we will simply act as though it were closed."

"Suppose they call Miss Freund at home?" Julia asked.

"She will simply answer with perfect rectitude that she doesn't know what they're talking about."

"Wouldn't she then immediately come round to see what they *are* talking about?"

"No doubt you are right. Call her up, Julia, and tell her enough to let her talk with confidence, but tell her to stay at home and grapple, if necessary, from there. Thank you, Kate, for coming. We bump, these days, from crisis to crisis. Like Pooh being dragged upstairs by Christopher Robin, bump, bump, bump. In fact, I think we can avert a real one-hundred-percent stinker in this case, if you'll excuse the expression, but the implications are terrifying. I hoped," she added to Kate, "that you might throw light."

"Where is Angelica?" Julia asked.

"Angelica is lying down in the nurse's office, being comforted by Mrs. Banister. You and she," Miss Tyringham said to Kate, "are our rescue squad. I hope," she rather faintly added.

"You want to know what's happened, of course," she continued. "We found a young man hiding out in the building almost unconscious with fright, worry, and near-starvation I suspect. But, for any of this to make sense, I'll have to explain all the complicated heaving and hoing we've been put to here to try to keep the school building safe from intruders. If you want to smoke, smoke. I'd offer you something to drink if I had it, but I don't. Will you be patient with me for a moment as I go through this rather long-winded explanation?"

Kate leaned back, lit a cigarette, and decided that if it were possible to wring anyone's interest to a higher pitch than hers was now wrung to, she didn't know what methods would have to be employed.

"I don't know if you've heard anything about some of the damage we've suffered in the building from intruders and thieves," Miss Tyringham began. Kate said that Anne Copland had told her about the stealing and the ruined gymnasium floor. "Yes; of course our first steps were to put up metal gates over all the lower windows and to secure the doors so that they were literally impenetrable with any device short of a major explosion. But the ways of today's intruders are many, varied, and ingenious. For one thing, however much of an eye we try to keep out—and we simply can't, for many reasons, have doormen guarding the lobby every moment of the day—anyone who puts his mind to it can gain entrance to the building and simply lie low until everyone's gone home. True, this takes a certain agility and dodging about to avoid the cleanup people, but I don't think it's past the ingenuity of even the most simple-minded robber. In addition, though it doesn't do to say so these days, our staff, both kitchen and cleaning, changes constantly for the most part—we have, of course, our old and faithful regulars—and one never knows what *their* motives may have been in taking the job. One is happy enough to find someone who will push a mop these days without being certain he was made for higher things: in short, very few questions are asked. Then there are the delivery men, plumbers, carpenters—well, I needn't go on endlessly with all the details; we have been damn lucky, actually, that nothing really untoward has happened in the school. Everyone was upset about the gym floor, of course, but it could have been a lot worse.

"Then," Miss Tyringham continued, "we acquired, blessed was the day, Mr. O'Hara, late of the United States Army, where he had been a sergeant with years of experience at guard duty. He liked the penthouse apartment we could offer him, and the small salary was no special problem since he has his pension and no one dependent on him. Forgive me if I seem to be going on at unconscionable lengths, but unless you have a picture of the setting, so to speak, you can't understand what happened.

"Mr. O'Hara moved in and he did keep a much better eye on things. He locked all the stairway doors, for one thing, and took both elevators up with him at night—he didn't mind walking down for the second one, he said; it was only up that he began to feel his years—and we seemed to be doing fine until the fire people discovered about the locked stairways and pointed out that, in case of fire, Mr. O'Hara would have no fast way out of the building except by leaping off the roof hopefully into a fireman's net (I do hope I have used the word 'hopefully' correctly, I can't bear to have it used to mean 'it is hoped,' such sloppy syntax) and of course we couldn't have Mr. O'Hara leaping off roofs, however hopefully, and it was then that he came to me with a proposal which seemed at first startling, but has turned out to be a most workable arrangement. He suggested dogs."

"Dogs?" Kate said. It was not what she had expected.

"Yes, my dear, dogs. Two mighty-vicious-looking Doberman pinschers which, however, Mr. O'Hara assures me, would never attack anyone. Their job, which they do superlatively well—so unusual these days, and, as Mr. O'Hara, who I fear is extremely conservative, pointed out, without demands, demonstrations, or strikes—is simply to make sure that nobody is in the building when it's closed. Nobody. Naturally, when I first heard the suggestion of dogs I said flatly that the thing was impossible—imagine two vicious dogs, however disinclined to bite, in the midst of a school of five hundred girls, not to mention the faculty, staff, parents, or cleaning people. The idea was ludicrous. But Mr. O'Hara assured me that department stores around the country have been using dogs successfully for years with no danger to customers or anyone else; the dogs are never let out except when there is no one in the building, or no one who has any business to be there, which is just the point."

"Where do they stay?"

"On the roof, my dear, next to Mr. O'Hara's penthouse. They have most elegant quarters, indoor pens and out, and Mr. O'Hara takes them for a run in the park very early every morning. I've been up to see them in their cages—of course, one simply must know everything that goes on in a school of which one is the head—and they stood behind their bars and bared their teeth at me in a quite properly terrifying manner. No one can get up to the roof, since the door off the auditorium is locked and there's a trap door at the top of the stairs as well. I expect I was finally won over to the whole idea because it's so absolutely uncanny—I mean, one could scarcely believe dogs were capable of so complicated an operation—I'll tell you about it in a minute—though of course one knows of seeing-eye dogs and all those sheep dogs of Hardy's and Lassie Come Home and all the rest of it.

"We installed electrified pads, one on the end of each hall, and when the dogs have been through all the rooms on that floor, and made certain there is no one in any of them, they press their paws on the electrified pad and it rings a bell in Mr. O'Hara's apartment. They make their way up and down the building during the night, and if they find an intruder, their job is to keep him until help comes, not to attack him unless he tries to run or to reach for a gun or something of the sort. Then they would leap on him, as I understand this— Mr. O'Hara offered to demonstrate with a man dressed in heavily padded clothing, but I decided to take his word for it as long as he was able to assure me that they were trained not to kill under any circumstances. Now, as you will readily have seen, if the dogs are cornering an intruder, they will not press their paws on the electrified pad at the end of the hall, and when he does *not* hear the bell go off, Mr. O'Hara, armed, one gathers to the teeth, goes to see what has happened. He lets the police know before going, on my insistence, and that's it."

"A neat system," Kate said. "I take it it's been a complete success."

"Complete. We haven't had a single robbery or intrusion, Mr. O'Hara thinks, because, however secret we may have been about the dogs, those who set about to make illegal entries know well enough that the dogs are here. We did have an unfortunate repairman, in the early days of the dogs, who agreed quite nobly to stay overtime to fix a leak in one of the lavatories, and no one thought to mention it to Mr. O'Hara. The dogs cornered the poor man, who fortunately simply stood in one place and trembled till Mr. O'Hara came and called the dogs off."

"Naturally," Kate said, "there are a million questions I want to ask about this fascinating arrangement, but I suppose I ought to contain my curiosity till we get to tonight's problem. I'm to gather that the dogs found someone tonight."

"They did. Angelica Jablon's brother, not to put too fine a point on it. The boy was in a dreadful state to start with, and when those two snarling beasts cornered him, he panicked completely and finally fell backward, striking his head on the corner of something. Of course he had a scalp wound which bled all over the place, scalp wounds always do; he's now in the hospital being treated for concussion and shock. He'll be all right, at least as far as tonight's little episode is concerned. Angelica, who saw him lying in a pool of blood, literally, I gather, before they took him to the hospital, is having hysterics down the hall in the nurse's office, being comforted, one fervently hopes, by Mrs. Banister. The dogs are back on the roof and the Theban is faced with another crisis. We are one over par this week."

Kate appreciated the light tones with which Miss Tyringham told this extraordinary story. From the point of view of the head of the school, it was vital to play down the drama—a boy had naughtily hidden out, been frightened by some dogs, and hit his head. An unfortunate accident; one did not wish to underestimate the human implications of his actions, but if there was any horror to being evoked by dwelling on the occurrence at the Theban, Miss Tyringham did not intend to evoke it. Kate could hardly blame her.

Yet, listening to Miss Tyringham, Kate was herself overcome with the sheer naked terror that boy must have felt. To hide out alone in an unlit building is to expose oneself to certain fears which the mind may explain away but the stomach responds to; to hide out as a criminal, it scarcely mattered why, even if his reasons were beyond question sound, could not be the calmest of undertakings. Then, suddenly, wholly without warning—for surely the dogs walk silently—to back away from two foaming monsters, well, not foaming, perhaps, but Miss Tyringham had said that they bared their teeth and certainly if he moved they growled. How was the boy to know they would not attack, and would he have been able to convey the news to his thumping pulses even if he had known?

Kate knew that not for many nights would she rid herself of that scene, imagined to be sure but probably not exaggerated. No wonder he had backed away, fallen, and hit his head—or had simply fainted with fear. Kate wondered if Miss Tyringham had considered the scene in this terrible way. For God's sake, Kate said to herself, of course she has; give her credit for the brains and imagination she's got.

"Now the reason we have called you, my dear," Miss Tyringham went on, "is because Angelica, after Mrs. Banister had quieted her down and when she was asked to explain the situation, attained coherent speech only long enough to compare herself to Antigone defending her brother. She howled that you were probably the only one who would understand *that*, and then refused or was unable to utter another word. So here you are, you see, rallying round."

"She hid the brother in the school building. What was he hiding from?"

"The United States Selective Service or his grandfather, probably both. What is clear enough is that he's determined not to be inducted. Not a new story to your ears, my dear, I know."

"And his sister was helping him."

"Yes. It was she, we assume, who thought of the dark and deserted Theban as the perfect hiding place. All the necessary sanitary facilities, heat, shelter, and food to be provided by the girls from the local delicatessen—I don't think they expected him to cook."

"They know about Mr. O'Hara, surely?"

"Oh, yes, but since he is over sixty, and one man, they never doubted he could be evaded. As he could have been, but for the unknown factor of the dogs."

"Do those miraculous dogs actually go into every room, including every cloakroom in the building?"

"Yes, that was one of the revisions we had to make in the routine when we instituted the dogs. The cleaning staff now leaves each door wide open—not that they know about the dogs. They would probably be frightened, and to no purpose."

"So I'm to talk to Angelica in the hope that she will grow calmer?"

"I trust it is not a forlorn hope. There is the problem of publicity, to which the Theban has always been highly allergic—but obviously of more importance is to discover how to deal intelligently with the whole terrible situation. Your great attraction, apart from the *Antigone* connection, is that you're from outside and supposedly not already prejudiced against the young and radical, not likely to assume a the-Theban-right-or-wrong attitude. And then, most people simply don't realize how difficult it is for adolescents to discover their own thoughts and feelings and attitudes when they are surrounded, as I fear Angelica is, either with those who agree with everything she says, or are horrified by everything she says. One wants a little toing and froing, if you follow me."

"And the brother is in a draft situation not unlike that of my nephew, with which I burdened you at our very first interview."

"Well, yes, my dear, that did occur to me. You can tell Angelica, quite truthfully, that you have met the problem before and sympathize. If, that is, you will be so good."

"What's the boy like, do you know?"

"Not the least bit. The family is, however, an unusual one. The father was killed in Korea just before Angelica was born, in 1953, and they have since lived with their grandfather, and they have been brought up by their mother, who is . . ." Miss Tyringham rearranged some papers on her desk as the great reticence of a headmistress overcame her, "shall we say a difficult woman, rather excitable and given to self-centered and frivolous pursuits. I don't think it's a happy family picture, which is one of the problems. Naturally, one wishes Angelica had not involved the school in quite so direct a way, but there is no question that we are, in any case, involved. This has been a very long-winded briefing. My apologies. Does Angelica strike you as . . . well, sufficiently level-headed to function when the chips are down?"

"I don't know. There's no good my saying I can answer that question, because the truth is I have no idea. She's worked well in the seminar, they all have, but . . . sorry not to be more helpful."

"On the contrary; it is precisely because of your lack of certitude that both Julia and I think you might do better here than Mrs. Banister. *Not* that there's any question of Mrs. Banister's support to Angelica through the last years; of course we had to call her when the band began to play."

"All right," Kate said, rising to her feet and trying not to look at the weary woman before her. "I'll see what I can do."

But it occurred to Kate, walking from the office, that in calling her Miss Tyringham had hoped for something—what, Kate did not know; neither, probably, did Miss Tyringham.

Neither, it soon became clear, did Angelica. She lay on the cot in the nurse's office, in a state close to comatose: bodily fatigue and emotional exhaustion had claimed her. Yet she seemed to have held off sleep till Kate appeared. Mrs. Banister, welcoming Kate with a nod, tiptoed from the room.

"Thank you," Angelica faintly said.

Kate sat down on the chair next to the cot. Angelica, moving one hand toward Kate but not touching her, closed her eyes as though some struggle had ended. Odd, Kate thought, how once or twice in our lives our presence, merely our presence, brings peace, and we can never know when the moments will be.

Sitting there, Kate sensed that her voice would bring comfort. Thoughts of Antigone and Angelica whirled in her mind, but would not settle into words.

"Wrong?" Angelica said. "Wrong to do?"

And then Kate thought, she would never know why, of Thornton Wilder's *Woman of Andros*. Well, it was a book about Greeks, after all. "Not wrong," Kate said. "The mistakes we make through generosity are less terrible than the gains we acquire through caution."

Angelica smiled and slept. Kate could see the tension leave her face. When the doctor arrived shortly after, Kate made her way back to Miss Tyringham's office, her mind full of questions about Angelica's brother. Fleetingly, Kate thought of the Greek gods and shivered.

Six

KATE reached home to find Reed almost invisible behind great piles of papers, which he said he was organizing, though his actions suggested rather that he was building himself a nest and planning to hibernate in it.

"Some people," Kate said, dropping into a chair, "hire an accountant or, when push has come to shove, a brother, like me."

"I have considered it," Reed said, examining some receipt with obvious astonishment. "Now, why should I have supposed I could deduct that?" he mused, moving the paper idly from one pile to another. "I even went so far as to consult an accountant reputed to save one more than his own fee in taxes. I soon discovered, however, that I had to get all the stuff together for him, which is by far the worst part of the job anyway, and that, furthermore, when one of those government computers spat forth my tax return in that unfair, happenstance way they have, I had to spend four hours a day for a week with the Internal Revenue people because I couldn't possibly afford to pay the accountant to go for me. I mean, my time may be worth as much an hour as his in theory, but not in cold cash. So, I bethought me, why pay him in the first place? How was your evening, speaking of unpaid hours?"

"If you really want to know, I'll tell you. The story begins with darkened lobbies and goes on through guard dogs who punch time clocks, becoming a bit emotional at the end with an interview with Angelica Jablon. How do you train a dog to press something with his paw? Before you answer, or I tell, I must get something to eat. I don't know why odd adventures always make me ravenous once they're over; probably a nervous response." They wandered together into the kitchen, and Kate, as she pottered around, told Reed all about the evening.

"They don't press a time clock with their paws as far as I know," Reed interjected at one point. "They stand with both front paws on the thing, which responds to their weight."

"Do you really think they could tell if someone was there, even hidden in a closet?" Kate asked.

"Oh, yes, I should think so. Dogs with a fine smeller and acute hearing would have little trouble with that—unless of course the closet was the size of a small baseball field."

"Don't all dogs have fine smellers?"

"They vary. Bloodhounds are the best. Dogs like salukis, Afghans, wolfhounds have very keen sight, for seeing great distances over the desert no doubt, but they don't have much sharper noses than a teetotaling woman who suspects her husband of having had a beer in the not too distant past."

"The things you know. I suppose there's a reason why they work in pairs."

"Much harder to diddle, much more threatening and powerful. A robber *might* try a pot shot at one dog, if he were hanging from the chandelier or something, the robber that is, not the dog, but it would hardly be worth the risk with two. What did you conclude from your talk with Angelica?"

"She was far too tired to talk at all, really. I *think* she was glad I'd come along, but she'd really had it. The problem is complicated by the grandfather, who, one gathers, has been a sort of father figure in the family, and of course the generation gap there is so enormous it's not a gap, it's a canyon."

"I thought grandparents and grandchildren were supposed to get on so well together, without the usual problems parents and children always have."

"That, I think, is only when the parents are actually there. In that case, the children and grandparents unite against a common enemy. But if the grandparents are in loco parentis, somehow all the old jollity doesn't work. I don't know which is more worrisome, really, the damage to Angelica and her brother or to the school. It does seem as though Miss Tyringham had had enough problems without this."

"But *this* is all part of the same problem, that damn awful war. Exactly what position was the boy in?"

"More or less the same as Jack's. At least, that's as much as I know, though doubtless there are simply reams of ramifications; there always are."

"Well," Reed said, "I'm sure you were a help, and perhaps she and her brother could hide out here if necessary. We can bring your nephew back, who will no doubt have some similarly circumstanced friends, and then the government can arrest us all for harboring draft dodgers. Sorry, you did say you hated people who looked on the bright side."

Kate, hungrily gobbling scrambled eggs, cocked a snook at him.

But, on the next day, Angelica showed up for the seminar and seemed in fair condition. The question of obedience, whether to the state or a father on the one hand, or to one's self or divine dictates on the other, was the question scheduled, with a pertinence that Kate found on the whole regrettable. Kate took her three minutes to inform them of a legal treatise on the subject by Daubé which discusses the problem of where obedience is due in connection with three great classical examples: Orestes, who kills his mother at Apollo's orders and is menaced by the Eumenides; Danaüs' fifty daughters, who have been ordered by their father to kill their bridegrooms on their wedding night and are thus torn between obedience to their father and to Aphrodite (the girls showed a certain inclination to discuss this case at exorbitant length, but Kate persisted in her introduction, subtracting discussion time from her three minutes, she having provided herself with a stopwatch for the purpose); and Antigone, torn between the decree of Creon and the laws of religion and familial love.

Alas, Kate continued, the knowledge that the problem of disobedience was older than one might have supposed did not make clearer where one's duty lay.

That, of course, was the whole point of Greek drama, if not of life, and Antigone is perhaps to be especially commended for having acted righter, anyway, than Orestes and the Danaids, except for the one among the fifty who took a fancy to her bridegroom and did *not* murder him. Her name, Kate concluded, her eye on the sweep hand, was Hypermnestra, if anybody cared.

Through all of this Angelica seemed much her usual self, if a bit subdued. The others entered into the question with their accustomed vigor, both Irene and Elizabeth defending the proposition that Ismene was quite right since she was like Antigone, a woman; it was not her business to give orders or disobey them. This point of view might have drawn more fire from Kate if the others had not leapt on Irene and Elizabeth with so much excitement that she had all she could do to keep order.

"And what," Angelica asked, "about Antigone's argument that she can never have another brother, so she owes him more than she would a husband or child who might, if they died, be replaced?"

"A really gross idea," Alice said.

"And spurious besides," Freemond said. She was their accepted Greek authority. "Anyway, Jebb says it's spurious, though I know Aristotle quotes it, and there's a good bit of disagreement. The point is, the whole thing doesn't make much sense, and it's certainly more Jesuitical than Antigone's usual arguments, which are quite straightforward and uncomplicated, no offense, Elizabeth, I hope."

"I don't think it's so complicated," Angelica said. "The point of what Antigone is saying, it seems to me, is that a woman can be anybody's wife or mother, but she can only be her brother's sister. It's about the only role a woman in Greece had that was ordained, so of course she felt she owed the brother everything." Her voice shook slightly, or perhaps Kate only imagined it. After a moment's hesitation, Kate brought the discussion back again to the conflict between the laws of state and of conscience. It was not merely a matter of the Greek dramatists, if that could be called mere. Socrates obeyed his god rather than the Athenians, Joan of Arc her voices, and Thomas More his religious beliefs. The Nuremberg trials considered this very point, and the soldier in a democracy who has been ordered to shoot into a crowd of demonstrating pacifists is not as recent an instance as we might suppose. Ought he to obey the law of the army or the law of the land?

"It always comes down to a matter of love, doesn't it?" Betsy asked. "Either you love someone or something enough to go out on a limb or you don't."

"Why did Antigone love her brother and not her sister?" Irene asked. "She couldn't have another sister either, could she?"

"But it wasn't a question of her sister's soul," Freemond said. "And some people think that she refused to let Ismene share her death in order to save Ismene's life."

"I don't believe it," Alice said. "She wanted all the glory."

"What's so glorious about being stoned to death, or walled up in a cave, if it comes to that?"

"At least it isn't *boring*," Alice sighed, with the weltschmerz possible only to the very young and the very old.

• • •

After considerable discussion, during which Kate was certain the particular case of Angelica's brother, or at least the question of civil disobedience in connection with the Vietnam War, would come up, the seminar disbanded without, in fact, touching on these tender spots. Kate decided that the girls, well aware of the contemporary relevance of the *Antigone*, had pitied Angelica and forborne.

Kate was sitting in the seminar room, wondering whether or not to go in search of Angelica, when a little girl knocked on the door and handed Kate a message, bobbing the curtsy of the young Theban girl. Kate thanked the child; the note, which was from Miss Freund, asked Kate to come to her office at the earliest possible moment. No doubt, Kate thought to herself, the dogs have nosed out someone else.

But the dogs hadn't. It had been Miss Strikeland.

She had noticed the same old man in the lobby again and, following orders, had notified Miss Freund. That lady now welcomed Kate to her office and presented the old gentleman Kate had observed on that earlier occasion. He had removed not only his hat but also his overcoat today, no doubt at Miss Freund's invitation, and was conservatively and expensively dressed, with a look of infinite sadness about him. Anyone less like a molester could scarcely be imagined.

"Miss Fansler," Miss Freund said, "this gentleman is Angelica Jablon's grandfather. He—er—wandered about the school, though as I told him, we should have been pleased to show him around. . . ."

"You're all busy," the man said, "with your work to do."

"Part of our job is to welcome parents and grandparents to our school. However, when I asked Mr. Jablon to come into my office today, he did finally ask if he might talk to you, Miss Fansler." Her faintly admonishing tone indicated clearly enough her opinion of Mr. Jablon's behavior, which had subtly contrived to move outside all regular channels.

Kate was inclined to agree with her. Her first reaction, as she later admitted to Reed, was selfish and inexcusable: for someone paid far from lavishly for conducting one seminar, she appeared to be taking on the most extraordinary interviews on behalf of the Theban. Her second reaction was to wonder if this wasn't going to be her brothers all over again, self-righteous patriotism and conservatism with the *Times* dismissed as a radical press and so on and so forth, impossible enough in one's brothers, but did one really have to take the whole matter up with old men who, after all, had a right to their own opinions if only they would keep them for their very own.

"Of course," she said, "but where . . . ?"

"I'm off to lunch anyway," Miss Freund said. "Use my office. If anyone asks for me, tell them to come back later."

Kate sat down warily in Miss Freund's desk chair, hoping it would confer some air of authority. She felt alarmingly silly.

"I ought not to take your time," Mr. Jablon said, "but you see, I am trying very hard to understand. It seems to me that the youth in this country have gone mad, they have . . ." Mr. Jablon's voice was rising, and he caught himself with the air of one who remembers, with difficulty, that he has come to inquire, not pronounce. Kate thought of Marianne Moore's phrase: "The passion for setting people right is in itself an afflictive disease."

"Was there something special you wanted to ask of me?" Kate suggested. Supposedly Mr. Jablon could discuss the problems of today's youth with anyone at the Theban, preferably those on a regular salary.

"It's about the play you're studying; Angelica has been telling me about it, saying there were the same arguments among the Greeks. I never had time to learn about the Greeks, but it always seemed to me that I would like to have my children study the Greeks, and their children, if they wanted to. It sounded so profound, the Greeks. Now I discover that your play is an excuse for betraying one's country, and that the hero of all this is a girl whose father murdered his father and married his mother, and whose mother was her grandmother too. Is that really great art?"

He sounded so genuinely outraged that Kate did not quite know what to say. It was the sort of conversation that could have been humorously recounted—the straight-faced retelling of famous dramatic plots is notoriously funny. Yet the farcical element was lacking here. Mr. Jablon not only thought that Oedipus was a dirty old man, he was unhappy about it.

"It was a question of destiny," Kate said. "Fate. For the Greeks, a man cannot escape his destiny."

"But that is what all these young people, with their dirty clothes and rioting, seem to be doing; they are trying to escape their destiny, which is to work and have respect for their elders and their country and learn something."

Kate sighed. "I know what you mean," she said. "If

they care for nothing but the moment, like hippies, what are they going to be doing when they're forty?"

"Yes," he said. "Yes. They should be preparing themselves."

"But that is your idea of destiny, not theirs. Oedipus thought he could run away from his destiny . . ."

"And they think they can run away from theirs."

"No. *You* think they are running away from what *you* conceive their destiny to be. But there are no oracles any more to tell us what is fated, or pleasing to the gods. There is no longer a Tiresias. You know, the play Angelica is studying was rewritten in modern times, similar in many ways, but without Tiresias. There is no one today who can tell us the truth."

"It is hard to be old," the man said. "My grandson, the boy who was found here . . . in earlier days, he used to talk to me sometimes, and he told me a line from Dante, another great writer I have never read: 'I did not die, yet nothing of life remained.' That puts it well."

"It seems to me," Kate ventured, "a great deal remains. Your grandchildren, your health, you have enough money. These things only seem insufficient when we have them, don't you agree?"

"What good is money today? So that my granddaughter can go to school and learn to sneer at authority? So my grandson can refuse to serve in the army of his own country? So that they can conspire against their own government? Even in little things. I can't take a walk at night, as I like to do; I will be mugged. I can't even walk during the day without being sickened by the garbage in the streets. I can't breathe the air. I have a car, an expensive car, but I can't park it on the streets, so what good is it to me; I can't go anywhere in it. If people still lived by the eternal principles . . ."

"Do you know what they are?"

"Everybody knows. They pretend they don't. They . . ." Again the old man stopped. He was beginning to get angry. "It can never be right to betray your country."

"Isn't the word 'betray' a loaded word? Can you 'betray' a democracy by disagreeing with the government in power?"

"Angelica told me some girls wanted to support the war here, and they were shouted down. She was proud of the fact."

"That is wrong, without question. That, I agree with you, is betrayal. But disagreeing about policy is not. Do you know who Dante put in the lowest circle of his hell?" It was not a rhetorical question, and Kate waited for an answer. The old man shook his head.

"Those," Kate said, "who betrayed their friends rather than their country." The old man shrugged as though to say he was not surprised; the education he had wanted for his children had turned out to be an illusion. The moderns, the ancients, none of them stuck by the old truths.

Kate, looking up, saw that tears had come to the old man's eyes, the helpless tears of age. He remained still until he had mastered them; he did not admit their presence.

"I don't know what I can say," Kate continued, after a moment. "I believe the *Antigone* is a great play. I don't think we agree on what are eternal truths, apart from the facts that man only learns at a terrible price and there are no easy answers."

"This is quite a school," the old man said. "I have spent several days in the lobby, just looking at it. Oh, it's very unostentatious, but so well run, so well organized. It is an old school."

"Yes," Kate said. "For an American school, it's quite old."

"It has always been a school for the best people," he said. "I know that. And now my granddaughter goes here. That is America."

"Yes," Kate said.

"I am a Jew," the old man said. "Do you know how I got to this country?"

"I know something about all that, in a general way," Kate said. But, she was thinking, he and my brothers are both so defensive about what they call America. Yet no doubt my brothers think America made a mistake in letting in the Jews. Patriotism makes strange bedfellows.

"My older brother, who was fifteen, came and earned the money for our passage. For my father and sister and me; my mother was dead. We brought our food onto the boat, the steerage, and cooked it over fires we made. I was six when I came here. My brother settled in New England, he worked in the mills. I went to school, and I didn't know any English. The boys brought their lunch—soup we used to bring in those days—and I remember there was a boy with a piece of meat in his soup. He made a face to throw it away, ach, soup meat, and I wanted that piece of meat so badly it was a pain. But I was too proud to ask. He tossed it away, into the dirt. I see it there yet.

"That's not the point," he said, shaking his head. "The point is this country. I went to work at fourteen;

I looked like a man. I went to college at night; I went to law school. I have been successful, and America made that possible. Shouldn't I feel gratitude toward my country, and loyalty? My grandchildren spit at America. What has your Antigone to do with that? Had her country given her such opportunities?"

"How many children do you have?" Kate asked.

"Two. My son died in Korea. He was *proud* to go. My daughter lives in California. I am seventy years old. My daughter-in-law is—an unhappy woman. So, sixty-four years after I come to this wonderful country, my grandson spits on the flag and my daughter hides him from the law. And you encourage this?"

Kate could not imagine what to say. Could she suggest that Haemon, Creon's son, argued with him in just this way, that Sophocles understood all this, that it was not new and did not spell the end of the world? Would he understand? Creon had many problems, but undue gratitude to Thebes was not among them.

"I have always been honest," the old man said. "I have never used my money for a bad purpose."

Her brothers liked to say that too. Probably it was true enough, in context. But what of the line from Proverbs: "He that maketh haste to be rich shall not be innocent"? Still, Mr. Jablon at least *had* made haste to be rich; he had not inherited the money which someone else had sinned to get, like Angelica, like her, Kate Fansler.

"I shouldn't waste your time," he said.

Kate shook her head. "You pay literature the honor of taking it seriously," she said, "but I don't know how to answer you. I want to pay you the honor of being honest. In that play, Creon does learn that he has been overcertain of the rightness of his decrees, that he has overestimated the importance of law and order. Of course, he learns it too late to save the life of his son, or his wife, or Antigone, all of whom die because of his stubbornness."

"Because life is cruel, does that mean he was wrong?"

"He knows in the end of the play that he was wrong. But I think it is only in plays that old men change their minds."

"So the young are always right?"

"I didn't say that. But today, with the question of this war, I believe they are not wrong."

"Well, you have been honest. My grandchildren shout at me. Do you think it is right that they should shout at an old man, at their grandfather?"

"I think it's an enormous compliment. It shows that they care enough about what you think to try and argue with you. I think you should be honored."

"That is not honor. One honors the old by treating them with respect."

"Well," Kate said, "we don't agree about that either. I'm not talking about manners in the formal sense. I'm talking about the exchange of ideas, the expression of feeling. I'm sorry. I haven't been any comfort at all, I know, but I haven't offered easy consolation. That would be easier."

"I wonder."

"Look," Kate said, "suppose you had asked for that piece of meat. Suppose you had eaten it, admitted your hunger, instead of remembering the meat lying in the dust. Would that have been so much worse?"

To Kate's surprise the old man shook his head, and

bowed it. She could see the tears again. "I'm sorry," she said, standing up. "I'll leave you."

"No," he said, rising. "Don't go. I ought not to get upset. I ought not to get emotional."

"Well," Kate lightly said, "we disagree to the last. I think you ought, when you've something to be upset about. Why else be human, why else love people?" She held out her hand to the old man. "Goodbye, Mr. Jablon. If you don't mind a good fight, come and see me again." And Kate, leaving the room, realized that she meant it.

"Which is all very well," Kate said later that afternoon to Miss Tyringham, "but I didn't mean to be quite as relevant as this. If only you had used a classicist who had muttered on about stichomythia."

"Poor Kate. And now Mr. Jablon has really put the lid on it. Of course, you're not as used to outraged parents as I am, and what doesn't make it any easier is that half the time you agree with them."

"That's it," Kate said. "There's nothing so uncomfortable as seeing both sides of a question. That's the *Antigone* for you, conflicting demands with right on both sides. The troubling thing about Mr. Jablon is that he's got a right to be conservative, if you see what I mean. He worked damn hard for everything and he's grateful for the chance to have been able to."

"And now he wants it all to be easy and frictionless. Oh, I've seen it often. What parents will so seldom understand is that love is hard work. Sexual love or other, and one thing we can say for this generation is that they admit there is another. Damn. I can tell we're in trouble here at the Theban by my daydreams. When I start playing with plans for a cottage somewhere in England where I can garden and fiddle in a string quartet with three other lost souls, I know things have come unstuck in a serious way."

"Dream all you want. You'd no sooner have settled in than they'd put up a development next door, or a power storage plant. I've seen it many times."

"I shan't run away yet. I'm really grateful to you for talking to Mr. Jablon; otherwise, of course, it would have been me. Everyone's very impressed with you around here, as far as I can see. Have you ever thought of joining the Theban in some permanent capacity?"

"Do you know what Dickens said when they asked him to stand for Parliament? 'I believe that no consideration would induce me to become a member of that extraordinary assembly.' That's the point of quotations, you know: one can use another's words to be insulting. Sorry, but if I can stagger through the next two months without falling right into the generation gap between Angelica and her grandfather, I shall fold my tent like the Arabs and as silently steal away."

The one who fell through that particular generation gap, however, was not Kate but Angelica's mother. They found her body at the Theban the following morning, and the secret of the dogs was a secret no longer, but communicated to the world.

The Theban had shut down for wars, protests against wars, in blizzards, and during strikes and power failures. Now it shut down for a criminal investigation.

Seven

"WE hope," Julia said, "to open the day after to-morrow. But, oh Lord, what a mess. Why couldn't that dreary woman have gone and panicked to death somewhere else? She was one of those phobic types, I understand, the sort who was afraid of everything—airplanes, fast cars, thunderstorms. One would have thought she could have had the decency to drop dead from fright on a highway somewhere."

"I gather," Kate said, "that decency wasn't her long suit."

"She didn't know the meaning of the word. Poor kids," Julia added, though whether she was referring to the Theban students in general, or Angelica and her brother Patrick in particular, Kate didn't know; it didn't seem to matter.

"Of course," Julia went on, "Mr. O'Hara is furious. He feels the integrity of his dogs has been impugned."

"Why on earth?"

"They didn't stop to notice her; maybe they thought she wasn't an intruder within the meaning of the act. There was a parents' meeting last night—that means the dogs didn't start their rounds until all the parents had gone. Then, apparently, the dogs went ahead and pressed their darling little paws where they should have. He says the body was dumped there this morning, after the dogs were back on the roof."

"Can't one tell when the body was dumped, or if it was dumped?"

"Can one? Perhaps Reed knows. Let's ask him; it'll give us an excuse to go upstairs and hover around the scene. I don't know how many more balls Miss Tyringham is going to be able to field," Julia said, reverting to her parental lingo, largely composed of outdated idioms. "You can tell she's thinking about that cottage in England more and more."

Gloomily, they began to make their way upstairs—stairs usually filled, at this hour, with rushing, laughing, shouting girls. The Theban, which demanded silence in the elevators, had long since realized the futility of requesting silence on the stairs. School discipline, where it succeeded, was a rare question of balance, and if one was fortunate, or clever, one won on the swings what one lost on the roundabouts. Because of the usual noise on the stairs it must, Kate thought, have been particularly eerie to creep up them in the vastness of the night—clearly one would be in a state of sufficiently heightened anxiety without encountering the hound of the Baskervilles and friend. But why on earth would the woman have come here—to see where her son hid out? One scarcely made such expeditions in the middle of the night. Besides, was she the sort of woman who would investigate the hiding place? From Julia's reports, she would have developed fifteen phobias at the very idea.

Suppose she had not come alone, or had been induced, enticed, enforced—could the other person have managed to arrive and depart between dog rounds? It seemed an outside chance, surely. Kate reminded herself that without even those meager facts the police were now collecting, all such speculation was foolish. Well, sensible, perhaps, in that it prevented the picture of that terrified boy and then the terrified woman from occupying her mind.

At the door of the room on the third floor, Kate found Reed. He was chatting with someone, no doubt a detective from the police force. Kate glanced quickly toward the room but saw nothing. "They've taken her away," Reed said. "I was just about ready to go in search of you. Hi." This last to Julia, whom he knew. "I guess I have something approaching information for your head lady."

"Do you want to see her now?" Julia asked.

"Is there anywhere we could get some coffee?" Reed asked.

"There's always a pot going in the faculty sitting room. With the school closed, the place might even be decently deserted."

It was characteristic of the Theban that, however great the need for space as the student body expanded, the faculty sitting room, which served no practical purpose whatever in the functioning of the school, was retained. It was an enormously comfortable room, filled with rather shabby easy chairs and a hot plate on which the promised pot of coffee pleasantly perked. Reserved for the faculty and never, no matter what the pressure, used for anything else, the room added greatly to the morale of the teaching staff. It was rumored around the Theban that the opinion of that room was a determining factor whenever the trustees chose a new head of the school. Anyone who found the room impractical (which it was) or space which could more obviously have been used for classrooms (requiring very little expenditure of funds for conversion) or a snobbish affectation, as though the Theban were an English college requiring a senior common room, cast immediate doubt upon herself as a suitable candidate. Such thoughts were considered to emanate from the sort of person who thought you should erect buildings in parks and hot-dog stands in national forests. But what good, Kate reminded herself, is morale in a school closed by a particularly horrible death? Parents had always been a problem to schools, certainly, but schools were not expected to deal with difficult parents by having them devoured, or anyway confronted, by vicious dogs.

"This is nice," Reed said. "I like your school and I hope it doesn't suffer too much from this mess."

"What we wanted to ask you," Julia said, pouring out coffee, "is if there is any chance the body was dropped here this morning, after the dogs were back up in their cage. That's what Mr. O'Hara insists, but then he's awfully defensive about his dogs."

"He's going to have to be," Reed said, reclining happily in a large chair and stretching his legs before him. "I'd like to go up and see them, by the way, but only after asking nicely and being invited. I've no official standing."

"Did you know those detectives?" Julia asked.

"Oh, yes. One does, you know. That's why I thought I might as well tag along. Besides, Kate was getting to look rather haunted, and I didn't want her to faint in a corner only to be discovered by those unfortunate dogs, who would never live *that* down."

Kate grinned at him. Indeed, the news this morning had rocked her more than she would have thought possible. She had great affection for the Theban, as one does for one's school if one has been happy there, but more than that she knew how all private schools and colleges were making their perilous ways on the thin line between financial and educational bankruptcy. She hated to see the Theban sacrificed to the peculiar fate of the Jablon family.

Miss Tyringham had telephoned at seven, not the crack of dawn certainly for someone connected with a school which opened its doors at eight-fifteen, but for Kate, a late riser, the bell appeared to be ringing in the middle of the night. She answered it, since Reed was showering (Tallulah Bankhead, when asked why she had never married, explained that all men rose early and took showers, which Kate, on marrying, was astonished to find true, however much it infuriated Reed to be referred to as "all men") and heard that there was a crisis. There was, indeed, a body.

"Mr. O'Hara discovered it this morning on his way downstairs," Miss Tyringham explained over the telephone. "Never mind how it got there, or if it died there. Perhaps your clever husband, with all his criminal experience, you know what I mean, can tell us. Anyway, the police doubtless will. Does your husband *know* the police personally?" she had gone on to ask with less than her usual finesse. Still, Kate thought, finesse under these circumstances would have bordered on the cold-blooded.

"Have you made sure . . ." Kate began, and then stopped. "Shall I come over now," she asked, "with Reed in tow if he hasn't fifteen unbreakable appointments?"

"My dear, would you? Julia is on her way. You both were here, really so comfortably *here* the other time, and this does seem so similar, alas, except of course that the poor woman is dead. First the boy and now his mother—they really are a most *unfortunate* family."

"But what on earth was the mother doing there—I mean, *she* wasn't hiding out, surely?"

"What she was doing here, my dear, is the whole point, I'm certain. But dead men tell no tales, unless the criminal investigation department can make them, if it is called the criminal investigation department. Mr. O'Hara says if they say the dogs did it they're not worth a tinker's damn, which is the nearest he gets to cussing before ladies, even under extreme provocation. In my more frivolous moments I used to amuse myself by wondering how he cussed in the army."

"Not with any words your fourth graders don't know these days, I assure you," Kate said. "We won't be long, I hope. Reed's shower has just stopped. I guess he only sang one show this morning."

"One show?" Miss Tyringham sounded pitifully willing to have the conversation achieve a note of lightness.

"He sings his way through Rodgers and Hart or Cole Porter. Occasionally Berlin or Kern, but only if he's feeling springlike, which he rarely is, even in spring."

"Tell him to sing 'June Is Bustin' Out All Over' for me," Miss Tyringham said. "Maybe it'll bust out sooner."

"He hates Rodgers and Hammerstein," Kate said. "Too gooey, too wholesome, and too many missing final g's. But I'll suggest 'Easter Parade' and he might feel near enough to the occasion to try that. I'll hang up now and see you soon."

It was all very well to try to pretend that life goes on, but when Reed and Kate had arrived at the school and talked with Miss Tyringham in the lobby, the sense of doom began settling over them like a cloud.

"Tell me what happened, from the beginning," Reed said.

"The police are upstairs now," Miss Tyringham nervously observed.

"Never mind. They're doing the usual routine, and waiting for the medical examiner. Who found her?"

"Mr. O'Hara. Will they remove her soon?"

"Oh, yes. As soon as they get pictures, measurements, and the rest. Go on."

"Mr. O'Hara called me at, oh, about six I guess. I was up as usual practicing the cello. He had taken the dogs out in the usual way. When . . ."

"What is the usual way?" Reed asked, ignoring the fact that Miss Tyringham's usual way was to play the cello at six in the morning. He had often pointed out to Kate that one of the most extraordinary aspects of murder investigations was the habits you discovered being practiced by the most conventional-appearing people. He supposed to so busy a woman, six o'clock in the morning provided the only undisturbed hour she could count on when she was not too weary from the demands of the educational world to hold the cello up between her knees.

"Very early in the morning he takes the dogs out for their run in the park. He takes them down in one of the elevators to distinguish this outing from business—I gather that's important with dogs. Seeing-eye dogs, I understand, are taken out for their personal tours by someone other than the blind person they lead. Not that that's either here or there. I have unfortunately noticed that one of the effects of the strain of all this is that I tend to go on, and on, and on. Perhaps," she added sadly, "it's age."

"Don't worry," Reed said. "It's your way of holding on in the dark, and not a bad way either. So he didn't see the body, one supposes, on his way down in the elevator."

"No, he did not. After the dogs have gone back up in the elevator, however, he brings down the second elevator and waits for Mrs. Shultz, who's in charge of the kitchen, to come, which she does at seven. He lets her in, and she runs him back up to the roof, and brings the elevator down again so that they are both on the main floor when the children and faculty arrive, the elevator operators having arrived in the meantime. I do hope that's clear."

"Perfectly."

"Good. *Then* he walks down having a final look at each floor and turning off the alarms on each floor."

"Can't they be turned off by a central switch upstairs?"

"That would have been expensive and, in any case, he fastens some sort of bolt on each one as he turns it off so that the children, should they bounce up and down on the darn thing, won't rattle it."

"I see."

"She was in the room—the body, I mean, Mrs. Jablon I should say—right across from the alarm on the third floor; it's an art studio, and the sun comes in in the morning. He couldn't miss seeing her, which was fortunate, considering what might have happened if he hadn't, if she'd been in some other room, and the children had all trooped in . . ." Miss Tyringham's voice trailed away at the impossibility of describing *that*. "As it was, you see," she went on, "we were able to call through and stop most of the children, and the ones who had left too early to get the message were turned back at the door with a vague story about breaking and entering. Not," she drearily added, "that I have any hopes of keeping this out of the newspapers. A body is a body, and in a schoolroom it's a damn bloody corpse—the adjective is vulgar, not descriptive: I gather from Mr. O'Hara that there was no blood."

"It may not be important," Reed asked, "but how in the world could you call five hundred children in what must have been well under an hour by then, or slightly fewer, I suppose, allowing for siblings."

"TAS," Miss Tyringham said, clearly happy to be back on familiar ground. "The Theban Alert System— it's been called TAS affectionately since long before my day. No doubt Kate remembers it?" She turned questioningly to Kate.

"Oh, my, yes," Kate said. "When there was a snowstorm one always hovered over the phone to see if TAS would call. If it didn't by eight, off to school you went."

"As you suggested," Miss Tyringham explained, "it would be close to impossible to call five hundred people, certainly in under an hour. And we must have an absolute rule that, if there is any question about the school opening, no one, no one, is to telephone to ask. We would simply have a swamped switchboard, Miss Strikeland would have hysterics, and everyone's phone would be so busy while they were trying to call that they couldn't be reached. If the school is to be closed for any reason, and I make such a decision in consultation with the section heads, four parents are called. They in turn each call three parents, one from each class, and these mothers now call others in her daughter's class, who call others, all pre-arranged. It works very well, though I'm not explaining it as clearly as I might."

"It couldn't be clearer. So you managed to close the school for the day, a wise decision. Then what happened?"

"It wasn't so much 'then' as 'meanwhile.' When Mr. O'Hara had called me, I told him to get in touch with Dr. Green as soon as possible, before calling the police, and to leave Mrs. Shultz downstairs to prevent anyone's entering the building except Dr. Green—that seemed sensible."

"I do admire people who can think clearly in a crisis," Kate said.

"Thank you for those kind words. Dr. Green came quickly; she's the school doctor and is used to our ways and devoted to the school. She realized immediately that she mustn't move the body, but she did make certain that the body was dead, something I have always thought to be rather difficult, unless one held a feather before the mouth like King Lear, and of course he was fooled even by that. But Dr. Green said not only was she positive, but rigor had set in, so the woman must have been dead some hours. 'You'd better call the police,' she said to me, 'and let them take over. There's no question of my signing a death certificate, even if I suspected what the woman had died of, and I don't. I don't want to move the body, which apparently doesn't appeal nearly so much to the police once it's lost its first fine careless rapture, but I don't *think* she was shot, or stabbed, or hit over the head. She may have been poisoned, but not by anything corrosive or cramp-inducing. Cheer up; she probably had a fit and died from natural causes', were her last kind words.

" 'But why here?' I of course asked. Dr. Green couldn't answer that, needless to say, so the police came and here we are. Julia as always came round and rallied. I don't know why I should have screamed in Kate's direction for help, except that she seems to have been rather involved with the Jablon family lately and—oh, I don't know, but I'm glad you're here."

"Don't worry more than you have to," Reed had said. "These things are like shouts from mountain tops, terribly loud and attention-getting at first, but dying down eventually to inaudible echoes."

"Time heals all, I know. Or at least covers it over with the scar tissue of forgetfulness. But, oh Lord."

And then Reed had gone upstairs to look at the body and talk with the police.

. . .

Now he sipped his coffee, leaned back yet further in his chair, and addressed himself to Julia's question.

"Could the body have been dumped here? I don't know what the medical examiner will find, but the answer is probably yes. It could have been. That doesn't mean that it was."

"Isn't it possible to tell if a body has been moved after death?"

"Sometimes. If there's been bleeding, so that the wounds correspond with the stains, if—oh, a hundred things—you can tell the body's been moved. But if I were to hit you over the head, hard enough to kill you but not hard enough to break the skin on the skull, say there," he pointed to Julia's head, "or if I were to press on one of the major blood vessels till all went black, or various other ghoulish things, once you were dead, if I picked you up and dumped you somewhere, I don't think medical evidence could necessarily discover it, unless, of course, I wounded the body after death. Wounds inflicted after death are identifiable as such.

"One should add," he finished up, putting his coffee cup down and wrenching himself with difficulty from the chair, "that moving a dead body is not all that easy. In fact, it's downright difficult. Apart from the fact that even in New York, where people sooner or later get used to everything, someone carrying a dead body, or even the body of an unconscious woman, would be bound to be noticed and remembered, if not commented upon. The point really is whether she was killed here or, as we still hope, died here."

"Any fascinating clues discovered by the police?" Kate asked.

"A few. For one thing, the victim had, in the pocket of her skirt, the label from a tie."

"A tie?"

"You know, a necktie, what those of us males who earn our living in the conventional world wear to work and even occasionally at other times. We know at least that whoever she was grappling with didn't go in for turtleneck evening wear, which surely tells us something. The label comes from a rather exclusive custom shirt shop on Madison Avenue, and will be looked into.

"Nothing in the room had been disturbed. She didn't back up, knocking over furniture and hitting her head the way her son did, which might mean anything, really."

"Including the fact that she was dead when she got to the room after the dogs were through."

"So you keep saying. But, if you want to get someone to the third floor of a building without leaving a trace, it is probably easier to get them there alive; certainly if you can think of a cock-and-bull story for getting them to walk the three flights, that's easier than carrying the body all that way."

"Was she heavy?"

"One hundred and thirty-five pounds, say, at a rough guess. She could be carried, but it wouldn't be easy. And she would have had to be carried at least some way on the streets, though I've already mentioned that. We're beginning to have circular conversations, which always happens in a crisis."

"Mightn't the middle of the night be a fairly safe time to tote a body around?" Julia asked.

"It might be, but in New York you can't count on it. Lots of tomcats come slinking home at all hours, not to mention lady cats. Plus all the people who work at night."

"Can you tell anything about the time of death?"

"Not all that much. The autopsy will tell us something, if we're lucky. If rigor had set in, as Dr. Green thought, that means she had been dead a certain length of time, certainly from before the dogs were through, probably five hours or more, but you'll never get any one medical expert on the witness stand to be absolutely certain about good old rigor, and if you do, someone will flatly contradict him. For one thing, the rooms are heated, which affects rigor, as does everything else under the sun."

"Will the police let us open the school tomorrow?" Julia asked.

"Oh, I should think so. And since there'll be so much buzzing and whispering and speculating, the sooner the routine gets back to something approximating the usual the better, I should think. Shall we go and confer with Miss Tyringham, if she's ready?"

As they started for the stairs and Miss Tyringham's office, the machinery of Homicide East moved into action. A detective set out for the custom shirt shop whose name appeared on the label found in the dead woman's pocket.

Eight

DETECTIVE George Young found that the custom shirt shop bore its name, "The Gentleman's Gentleman," discreetly upon the door. When Young entered, there was a customer in the shop, and he waited patiently until the customer concluded a, to Young, unbelievably protracted discussion of shirt cloth, stripes, cuffs, and colors. Young himself, when he needed a shirt, wandered into some store, named his neck and sleeve size, and walked out almost with the first thing he saw. He supposed the rich had more time and didn't mind spending it this way, not to mention money, though money was not mentioned between the gentleman's gentleman and his customer. The owner of the store, pausing for a moment in his momentous deliberations, and apparently sizing Young up as unlikely to be a very remunerative proposition, asked if he could do something for him. "I'll wait," Young said, in a voice indicating he intended to.

When the customer had at last exhausted all alternatives, decided upon his shirts, and retired, Young approached the counter, flipping open the case which held his identification. "We have a label from your shop found under circumstances of interest to the police. We wonder if you can help us. The owner of the shop is a man named Sam Meyer. Is that you?"

"Yes, but I don't see how I can help you. I have many customers. As most of them are well-to-do, when they tire of their shirts they give them away, perhaps to their servants. You see the problem."

"Did this label come off a shirt?"

Mr. Meyer glanced at it. "No, that's off a tie. They're even given as gifts. I'm afraid I can't be much help."

"Try. Do you have a customer named Jablon?"

Mr. Meyer looked concerned. "Mr. Cedric Jablon is one of my oldest customers. Is that whom you mean?"

"Let's talk about him and see."

"I met Mr. Jablon years ago, when I was a salesman at a big chain of elegant men's stores when I began, and Mr. Jablon used to get his suits and all his accessories from me. When I left to open this shop, he came to me for his shirts. He couldn't be mixed up in anything the police had to do with—it's impossible."

"Did Mr. Jablon's grandson ever come in for a tie?"

Mr. Meyer eyed Young uneasily. "Look, I don't want . . ."

"Just answer the question."

Mr. Meyer sighed. "The old gentleman brought the boy in, oh, perhaps a year or two ago, to have some shirts made for him. Made rather a thing of it, you know, now the kid was grown and Grandpa was going to give him some fine shirts. But it didn't turn out that way."

Young, impassive, continued looking at Mr. Meyer.

"This younger generation," Mr. Meyer said. "The boy asked me the price of the shirts—it was fifteen dollars then, which it was worth, considering each shirt is individually tailored and made of the finest Egyptian cotton; they're over twenty now—and when he heard the price he became, I regret to say, rude. He said it was a crime to spend money like that when there were kids being bitten by rats in the ghettos." Mr. Meyer shuddered, at the recollection of the whole scene, which clearly had reached traumatic proportions in his mind, and particularly at the unforgettable mention of rats in his exclusive and elegant shop. "I pointed out to the boy, though perhaps it was not my place to do so, that I too had begun in a ghetto—that the word, in fact, was invented for Jews who were not allowed to live anywhere else—that I had worked to get here, and that if he wanted to fight rats in the ghetto he did not have to insult me before beginning. I became angry, I'm afraid, and I called up later to apologize to the grandfather, Mr. Jablon, but he was nice enough to say he didn't blame me, and that he wanted to apologize for his grandson. Did you find the label in Harlem?"

Young, who had come to ask questions not to answer them, ignored this. "Your labels haven't changed any?" he asked. "There's no way of telling what year the tie was sold?"

"None," Mr. Meyer shortly said, obviously feeling he

had spoken too freely and would henceforth confine himself to monosyllables. "Of course, if you had the tie . . ."

"Right," said Young. "Be prepared to sign a statement setting forth what you told me."

"Oh, dear. It's all true, of course, but I don't want . . ."

"Don't sweat it," the detective said, and was gone.

Mr. Sam Meyer, the gentleman's gentleman, waited a few minutes, perhaps to see if the detective would return, perhaps to make a decision. Then he picked up the phone and dialed.

The medical examiner, meanwhile, had completed his work. There were still more refined tests to be done on some of the organs, and a specialist in cardiac pathology would have to be consulted before any official report could be made, and there was always room for later indications which might affect the detailed diagnosis but, the M.E. reported, and the officer at Homicide East, who knew Reed, passed on the information: Esther Jablon had died of a heart attack. She had died, though naturally they would not put it so close officially, sometime between nine and eleven the previous night. Certainly, the officer told Reed, she might have been stricken earlier, but she did not actually die much earlier. There was no way of knowing if the body had been moved after death, but there were no special indications that it had.

There would have to be a long conference with the victim's physician—that was set up for late today. But there seemed no question that the dead woman had suffered from a genuine heart ailment, even while she was extremely hypochondriacal and a nervous wreck generally. Were the symptoms congruent with her having been scared to death by two vicious-looking dogs? Certainly they were. Any evidence of drugs, liquor, et cetera? She had had a drink, probably before dinner, not enough to make her drunk. She had eaten two to three hours before dying, so if you can, find out when she had dinner; we're working on it anyway. She had recently taken a tranquilizer, meprobamate; according to her doctor she took them regularly; she also had sleeping pills on her bathroom shelf next to the meprobamate, but she had not taken one before her death. Death must have been fairly rapid. So it was really true that someone could be scared to death? Oh, yes, given all the proper conditions of the heart and so forth. Things were kind of humming around here now, but would Reed be sure to call back if he wanted any further information—sure, Reed would be the first to know if the additional tests or the woman's doctor revealed anything of interest. See you around.

"Which doesn't get us much further," Reed said to Miss Tyringham that evening as she sat in the Amhearst living room sipping a brandy. "What it will come down to, I'm reasonably certain, if you play your cards right, is that it will be decided she was killed by the dogs, just seeing them, that is. If you're lucky, you may even get away without a case at all, unless the insurance company acts up."

"Why should the insurance company act up?"

"If the Jablons sue you for enough money, it may be

worth the insurance company's while to try to prove that she was the victim of some involved nefarious plot. Will the Jablons sue you?"

"I very much doubt it. I spoke to old Mr. Jablon only briefly, to offer condolences and inquire about Angelica."

"How is Angelica?" Kate asked.

"Very bad, I regret to say. This, coming on top of the incident with her brother, has been too much. She has apparently become morose and silent, having first been hysterical. They have put her in the hospital. Mr. Jablon knew about the dogs, of course, because of his grandson's experience; he felt it very foolish of his daughter-in-law to have gone to the school, and he certainly didn't mention suing."

"Some lawyer may yet get hold of him; it's a case with infinite possibilities."

"I doubt a lawyer could persuade Mr. Jablon to do something he didn't want to do," Kate said. "But one can't be certain what he may decide is owed him. He seemed to hold the school responsible for Angelica's radical opinions, and he may sue in general outrage at the *Antigone* seminar. I hope not."

Miss Tyringham leaned back in her chair and twirled the brandy snifter around in her hands. "Let me put a supposition to you, and when I finish, give me your reaction." They nodded their agreement with this.

"Let us suppose," she said, "that everybody concerned accepts the explanation you have just indicated. That, for reasons we will never know since she is dead, Mrs. Jablon went to the school, somehow gained admittance and, around midnight, was confronted with two Dobermans, became terrified and, having a heart ailment, died of a heart attack brought on by extreme fright. Suppose that—let me be absolutely blunt here—suppose that using all the influence the Theban could muster, and frankly that is an impressive amount of influence, we could get such a verdict. The whole case is dropped, greater precautions are taken about the dogs; perhaps we will have to get rid of them altogether. Gradually, the whole thing is forgotten, and the school continues on its perilous way in these difficult times. Would you be satisfied?"

"We?" Reed asked. "Kate and me?"

"Yes. You. You two."

"Satisfied in what way? Miss Tyringham, some years ago a society woman in New Jersey shot and killed her husband as he entered her bedroom, nude, in the middle of the night. She claimed that she thought he was a housebreaker. There was evidence the two had not been getting on too well. A jury of twelve good citizens and true acquitted her of murder in the first *or* second degree, and turned in a verdict of accidental death. We all forget about that and we can all forget about this. Suppose they had decided it was murder, premeditated or not? What would have been the good? Her children would not only have been fatherless, they would have had a convicted murderer for a mother. She wasn't likely to go on and shoot anyone else; quite the contrary. Vengeance is mine, saith the Lord."

"It seems to me," Miss Tyringham said, "that what is monstrous about your story is the sense of the law bending with the prevailing winds. Surely the young are right: if we are going to fret and scream and thrash about because the streets are not safe, nor even our houses, and heaven knows they are not, we must be certain that we do not demand for the criminals a retribution, law and order if you like, which we do not follow through on—shall we say among the three of us—for the upper classes?" She sipped her brandy.

"Exactly," Reed said. "I'm an old cynical hand at all this, and have learned to blink at many things. Ask Kate; she's still honorable, naïve, and interested in the death of Roland. Ask her if she would be satisfied with the happy ending you outline for us. One of my troubles, you see, is that I have some sympathy with the kids."

"Which I share," Kate said with feeling. "My brothers, who always stand for the hard hats of the world when I become heated and incoherent, talk about law and order all the time, I mean *all* the time—crime in the streets, the number of burglarized homes, campus unrest, the police have no power, no respect for the law, blah, blah, blah. But if I point out that even the ocean has become polluted with oil slicks, that the automobile manufacturers won't make bumpers that protect cars because they can better sell bumpers that are only decorative, that the drug companies wanted to market Thalidomide and so on, he—whichever brother I'm talking to, that is—doesn't get heated at all, he doesn't even give more than a token tsk tsk. Does all this have anything to do with what we're talking about?"

"It does, in a way," Miss Tyringham said, "that is, if we're talking about honor, which perhaps we really ought to do a bit more, meaning honor, not face, which is what most people who use the word 'honor' mean. Still, I must think of the school; that is my job. And, for the sake of the school, we must perhaps assume, if they will let us, that the whole thing was an unfortunate accident. Perhaps it was, you know."

"Is there really any chance of a cover-up?" Kate asked. "Would the police really let the whole thing lie, like sleeping dogs, to use a singularly appropriate cliché?"

"Yes," Reed said, "I'm afraid there's a very good chance, if no claims are made. She did die of a heart attack, assuming they don't find anything more sinister in further examinations. What's the point of offending a lot of important people, when the only ones who may be unfairly accused are a couple of dogs who, at worst, will be retired to the country or put on another job? In the end, we are all sensible men who understand one another."

"So you are satisfied?" Miss Tyringham asked him.

"Satisfied? Compliant, rather. How could one be satisfied? The number of unanswered questions is staggering: How did she get into the building? Why should such a woman go to such a place, which is most unlikely from all we know of her? Why did she have that label in her pocket, the case's only tangible clue?"

"Was it off a tie you've been able to trace?"

"Easy as pie. Grandpa's been buying his ties there for years."

Reed began to walk around the room. "Why, to continue acting the elephant's child, did she repeat her son's terrifying experience? Why is the school involved at all? Could it be, to take a random shot, that Mr. Jablon thought the school deserved to meet real trouble instead of encouraging their students to be unpatriotic? Was he willing to sacrifice his daughter-in-law, whom perhaps he didn't care for, to such a fate? I could go on spinning off the questions for hours."

"Exactly," Miss Tyringham said. "But you haven't really answered *my* question, nor has Kate."

"I have never believed," Kate said, "that one should stop in the middle of an inquiry because one doesn't care for the way the problem is working out, or because it is too demanding to go on. Surely that's the mark of a slovenly and unscholarly mind, if not worse. People's unwillingness to accept the consequences of their acts—allowing rivers to become polluted, to take an impersonal example—seems to me horrible. Like the cigarette companies' hiring people to prove smoking doesn't cause cancer. Oh dear, I've wandered off again."

"One can't stop in the middle," Miss Tyringham said, "but one could decline to begin."

"Once you've asked the question, you've begun," Kate said. "Anyway, even if we found an answer, we wouldn't necessarily have to do anything about it, would we?"

"There, I think, you would be fooling yourself," Reed said. "I can promise you, both of you, that if you ask one more question, investigate one more occurrence connected with that night, you will be in it up to your necks, without a foothold. If you want to stop, stop now."

There was a silence of several minutes.

"We had better begin," Miss Tyringham said, "by trying to find out what went on in the Jablon household that night. Perhaps the grandfather not only knows, Kate, but will tell you."

"Also," Kate said, "we'd better find out how those dogs work—I mean, actually ask to see them on the roof and all. Surely Mr. O'Hara won't object if we succeed in exonerating the beasts."

Reed stared at them a moment and then, with a massive sigh, refilled his glass.

The next morning, accordingly, found Kate and Reed at the Theban to keep an appointment with Mr. O'Hara on the roof. He had agreed, with very poor grace, to see them. "I've told it all to the police, and I'm not telling it to you again to have you telling me those dogs brought on anyone's death." It was only by insisting upon their unswerving belief in the innocence of the dogs that Kate and Reed were admitted onto the roof at all.

"Kitto," Kate reported as they made their way upstairs, "who is one of the best commentators on the *Antigone*, says: 'With the first entrance of the Watchman begins that part of the play which is most full of difficulties.' How true, O muse, how true."

"Sheridan Whiteside," Reed retorted, "when he comes on the stage says: 'I may vomit,' which seems to me on the whole a far more appropriate quotation."

They waited in the auditorium for Mr. O'Hara. Kate rather uneasily wondered if he would appear like Heathcliff with snarling dogs at his heels, but he was quite alone and even greeted Reed with mild cordiality. He seemed to find Kate, another female in an institution already overflowing with them, superfluous, and waited with undisguised hope for Reed to bid her adieu at the doorway to the roof.

"Have to have Miss Fansler along, you know. I promised," Reed said. "But she'll be very quiet and only ask intelligent questions. She's really quite well behaved."

"They have lady district attorneys now, then," Mr. O'Hara asked, "or she's connected with the school?"

"She's connected all down the line, but she's a proper female and always walks six paces behind. Lead on."

Mr. O'Hara, with a grunt of annoyance, passed through the door first, holding it for Reed but pointedly not holding it for Kate. They immediately climbed the steep though short flight of stairs to the roof, and once they had climbed out on it—Reed helping Kate while avoiding O'Hara's eye—O'Hara closed a trap door which, flush with the roof, fitted neatly over the stairs.

"You see," he growled, "the dogs can't possibly get downstairs during the day, as some idiots have been suggesting, even if they could get out of the cage, which they can't. Obviously. Females have eyes but I sometimes wonder if they can see with them, let alone think."

"An army man, aren't you?" Reed asked. "Too bad about it's being a girl's school."

"Everything was fine until that pansy boy hid out here to avoid defending his country. It's a good job. I was not complaining." Kate thought of mentioning that Achilles had hid among women, but decided against it. If Mr. O'Hara had heard of Achilles, which seemed doubtful, he probably considered him a slacker and a sorehead, or worse.

"Dogs this way," O'Hara said, "and they'll growl at you, so if you plan to scream, don't. You can wait here."

"Miss Fansler never screams unless you pinch her," Reed said. "She's trying to prove the honor and loyalty of the dogs, you know, and to demonstrate that their training held good, so I really do think we ought to encourage her. Good God!"

This last admiring outburst was inspired by the two Dobermans, which stood together in their cage, lightly baring their teeth and growling in a quiet, anticipatory sort of way. Their cage was large, allowing them room to run up and down a bit, should they so choose; connected to the cage was a small house into which, one gathered, they retired to shelter from the elements. Now they stood side by side eyeing Reed and Kate with a suspicion largely tempered by the presence of Mr. O'Hara. "All right, my beauties," he said. "Lie down and have your naps."

"Have they names?" Kate asked.

"No questions or I'll take you home," Reed whispered.

"Certainly they've got names," Mr. O'Hara said. "This is Rose and this is Lily. Give us a kiss, now." And the astonishing Mr. O'Hara, whose misogyny evidently excluded the canine breed, bent near to the fence, stuck a finger through the wire and scratched the ferocious beasts, which, Kate and Reed noticed, kept a wary eye on them even as they accepted these loving overtures. But their hackles were down, their coats again sleek.

"How would they react if you weren't with us?" Reed asked.

"Walk away a moment, let me pop into my house, and find out. But don't stick any part of you through that fence." Kate and Reed stepped back onto the trap door as Mr. O'Hara vanished into his apartment, which, apart from a water tank, some mechanism for the elevators, and the dog cages, was all that stood on the roof. The view of the city was unusually open; indeed, Mr. O'Hara had found himself a fine spot.

When he had disappeared, Kate and Reed walked toward the cage. The response of the dogs was instantaneous and ferocious, but they did not bark. "They work quietly, one gathers," Reed said. "Even the most besotted dog lover, discovering himself in the company of these beasts, would have a heart attack it seems to me. But we better not say so to friend O'Hara."

"If he dislikes females so much, human that is," Kate said, "perhaps he took the job and talked Miss Tyringham into the dogs just to give women's education a bad name; had you ever thought of that?"

"Nonsense. He's the sort right out of Dickens, who probably has a little girl who's the apple of his eye, or wishes he did. Like his dogs, he growls but does not bite."

"So," Kate darkly said, "we are supposed to believe."

"Well, we can't stand here talking; he'll think we're conspiring against him." The dogs watched them walk toward the house, their growls rumbling in their throats.

"Satisfied?" O'Hara asked.

"Thank you," Reed said. "Do you mind if we ask you a number of silly questions? That's the name of the game, I'm afraid."

"The police have already asked me."

"Of course they have. But we would rather not believe the dogs are to blame, which sets us off from the police and makes us distinctive and interesting. What time do the dogs begin their rounds?"

Mr. O'Hara, with a sigh Kate recognized as the sort she was wont to draw when she found herself trapped into a cocktail party, dropped into a chair, invited them to do likewise with a barely gracious wave of his hand, and began to make a great business of lighting a pipe.

124

He did not answer until they were all surrounded with clouds of smoke.

"Smells lovely," Kate said.

"I'll join you if I may," Reed said, taking out his own pipe. Mr. O'Hara's scowl deepened.

"Ordinary days," he said, "I let Rose and Lily out on their rounds about eight o'clock, when I've finished my supper."

"Cook for yourself?" Reed asked.

"Of course. What do you think I've got, a blooming maid?"

"I thought perhaps you got food from the school kitchens."

"Cottage cheese," O'Hara said.

"And wet tuna fish," Kate added. Reed glared at her.

"What do you mean by ordinary days?" he asked.

"When they aren't planning some blooming fling," he said. "Dances, meetings, and the like. A school's a school and ought to steer clear of all that nonsense, but they hired me to guard the place, not to run it. *Those* nights I don't get the doors shut and the last of them out till nearly eleven."

"Do the meetings run that late?" Kate asked.

"Over at ten-fifteen on the nose; Miss Tyringham is very clear about that. But of course the ladies stand around the halls gabbing away, and if it's raining the men, poor slobs, have to try to get cabs, and one thing and another, it's damn near eleven before the last of them is out of the building and on her way."

"Do you wait down there to see them off?"

"I do. I'm there to see them in, too. Has to be someone, or you might have anyone wandering in, now wouldn't you?"

"Is any real check kept on who enters?" Reed asked.

"Naturally; we are not a public theater. I know the teachers, to look at anyway, and the teachers know the parents."

"All the same," Reed said, "if two people, a man and a woman of the right age, and looking right, were to wander in, I bet they could even attend the meeting. The teachers can't all know all the parents. If there's a perfectly acceptable couple there, is anyone likely to confront them and say 'Name your daughter or abandon these premises'? One assumes they're somebody's belongings and lets it go at that."

"Not quite," Kate said. "The Theban is more organized than it looks to the casual eye. You are asked to say if you're coming to meetings, in the first place. Admittedly, someone might neglect to send back the form, or to telephone, or she might say she wasn't coming and then discover she was. But, you see, each parent has a name card with that new sticky stuff that sticks to clothes without leaving a mark. It says, for instance, Mrs. or Mr. Fred Jones, Esmeralda II, Sylvia IV, and each parent sticks that on when she arrives. The box with the correct tags is already out and waiting for the parents having the meeting, and everyone sticks on a tag, the theory being that even if there's a mama or papa whom everyone doesn't instantly recognize, she would hardly be likely to stick on Mrs. Jones's tag when she might sit next to someone who knows Mrs. Jones perfectly well, or Mr. Jones if a man. I do hope you're following all this."

"Like all the Theban arrangements, it is simpler to work than to describe; I still say that if someone made herself a tag saying Mrs. Montmorency, no one would challenge her. Everyone would assume she belonged. It's something to keep in mind anyway. Let's say an eye is kept for interlopers. Sorry to interrupt you, Mr. O'Hara, but we have to get everything straight and in order. Do go on."

"With what?" Mr. O'Hara growled, with a rumble in his throat that was reminiscent of Rose and Lily.

"It's eight o'clock on ordinary days, eleven on meeting days, and then you let the dogs out on their rounds."

"I didn't say I let them out on their rounds at eleven, I said that's when everyone's left the meeting. I go up and check the floors where the meeting's been, and straighten up a bit, open the doors and all that. Then I take the elevators up and *then* I let the dogs out."

"What about the tour you make through the building after the cleaning staff has left," Kate asked, "opening doors and so forth?"

"I've already made that, same time every day. When there's to be a meeting, I leave one of the elevators down, that's all. I have to run that to take up the parents and all."

"Suppose," Reed asked, "one of the parents, or someone passing herself or himself off as a parent, were to hop upstairs and hide out after the meeting?"

"The dogs would find her. Or him. That's what they're there for. If I was to keep going through the building all night, I wouldn't need the dogs, would I? And I can't smell everyone out and they can."

"Without question?"

"Yes, damn it, that's what I've been telling them—the police, the school, Miss Tyringham, everyone asks the same blooming question. If that crazy dame was in

127

the building hiding out, the dogs would have found her. She wasn't there."

"She was found there," Reed said.

"I know she was, damn it. I found her. Someone dropped her body there after the dogs had finished, either when I had them out for their run, or when they were already upstairs."

"Mr. O'Hara, rigor mortis had set in. At the time your dogs were out for a walk, she was as stiff as a statue, all in one piece like a hunk of marble. Do you really think someone could carry a life-size statue into this building in the morning without being seen, coming or going?"

"They did it, that's all I know. You can break the joints in rigor mortis, can't you? In the army . . ." He became aware of Kate's presence and stopped.

"You can, though hardly all the joints. However, they didn't. That is, there rigor was, unarguably."

"Well, she wasn't in the building hiding out, or the dogs would have found her."

"As you keep saying. Suppose she was in a large room with the door closed."

"They would have known it. They would have waited outside until I came, having missed the regular signal. Besides, if she was shut up in a room, how did they scare her to death? Why don't you try hiding out and see?"

"Try what?"

"Hide in a room. Just stand in it and see what happens. Try to hide out where they can't find you. I'll know when they've found you, and I'll come. You won't be hurt if you just stand there. Try it. Hide out in the coziest place you can find. Those dogs, damn it, are as perfectly trained as West Point cadets, and they don't ask questions."

"How will you know when they've found Mr. Amhearst?" Kate nervously asked.

Mr. O'Hara positively snarled. "I've been telling you. The alarm won't go off, and I'll know they've cornered something when it doesn't and I'll go and see. It's the safest and most secure protection there is."

"Do you listen for the alarms in your sleep?" Kate asked.

"I sleep in the day if I'm given a chance," Mr. O'Hara growled.

"We shall take the hint," Reed said, rising and knocking out the tobacco from his pipe into Mr. O'Hara's already filled and odoriferous ashtray. "May I get in touch with you if I decide to play the tethered goat? Thank you, and please say goodbye to Rose and Lily for me."

Mr. O'Hara tramped out and lifted the trap door for them. "Push the bar on the door at the bottom," he said.

"Thank you, Mr. O'Hara," Kate said in her best Theban manner.

Mr. O'Hara growled.

Nine

THE following morning the Theban opened with an assembly for the whole school. The rumors of the body and the dogs had swept through the student body like wind through a field of grass—Kate remembered that Midas' wife, unable to keep the secret of her husband's ass's ears, had whispered it to the reeds by the river, who had spread the news; the metaphor in that old tale went right to the heart of rumor.

It was rare to have an assembly for the whole school in the middle of the year, but Miss Tyringham had recognized the need for some forthright statement, something which joined the students, even the littlest ones, with her in a sense of community. The babies from the kindergarten filed into the front row and sat, their eyes shining at Miss Tyringham, who stood in her gown at the podium, and their silence, the silence of the whole audience, was palpable, like a heartbeat pounding in the ears.

Since it was a morning assembly, they began by singing a hymn: "Once to every man and nation comes the moment to decide, In the strife of Truth with Falsehood, for the good or evil side." They sang with vigor, as though confirming something, and sat down with a rustle of anticipation. Miss Tyringham spoke:

"You will all know, without my having to tell you about it, the reason for this assembly. Our school has suffered an accident of the sort that gives rise to all kinds of speculation. What has, in fact, happened is that a woman, the mother of one of our seniors, Angelica Jablon, was found dead in the school building in the early morning two days ago. We know that she died of a heart attack; she was not killed by violence of any sort. We do not know for certain whether or not she was frightened by the dogs which, as you now all know, patrol the school building at night.

"I am not going to pretend to you that we understand all the ramifications of the death. We do not know what she was doing in the school building, what she was seeking here. We shall do our best, with the help of the police and private investigators, to learn as much of the truth as we can.

"You will all understand that for the sake, not only of the student involved and her family, but also for the sake of the Theban, rumor and gossip *must* be firmly and quietly discouraged. Of course, people will ask you about 'the body at the Theban.' You must answer as briefly as possible, and go on to something else. Do not, I suggest to you, use this occurrence as a way to gain attention. It is often possible, at the price of loyalty and discretion, to become momentarily the center of attention, but the price you pay is, I am sure you will agree, too high. The Theban and the family involved will survive this sad occasion the more readily with your help. I have myself complete confidence in your good sense, which is why, contrary to much advice, I have welcomed this opportunity to take you into the confidence of the school, and to provide you with all the information I, and the faculty and trustees, have. We will now sing the closing hymn, 'O God, Our Help in Ages Past,' and I remind the youngest girls that we wait in our seats until the singing of the Dresden Amen and *then* file out."

She nodded her head briskly, and the piano struck up the opening chords.

"I hope to God she knows what's she's doing," Julia said to Kate in the doorway of the auditorium.

"I think she's right," Kate said. "It's always better, when you come right down to it, to trust people rather than to try to outwit them. Particularly when they will discover your secret anyway and then feel a proprietary right to it."

"Oh, she had to tell them, of course," Julia said. "But why not let the whole thing rest there? Blame the dogs and go on with our routine."

"I wonder if we should use even dogs as scapegoats."

"I don't mean to drive them over a cliff, you know."

"The fate of the goat never troubles me as much as the fate of those who burden it with their sins. Sorry, I don't mean to sound ponderous—I'm as troubled as you are, and now, of course, Reed is planning to let those damn beasts corner him to see what happens. Needless to say I'm full of high principles until my husband decides to put them into action. I have never cared for medieval romances, as opposed to epics, and did not know I was marrying a knight of the Round Table."

"Good God, Kate, I don't think he'll actually . . ."

"Oh, yes he will, he's as stubborn as a mule when he makes up his mind about something. I'm sure there's something more stubborn than a mule that he's as stubborn as but I don't know what it is. He says, of course, that the dogs are perfectly trained, that he's seen guard dogs work, that he will wear padding, that he's in no more danger than in driving on any highway, which is hardly consoling. Meanwhile, there are the Jablons."

"He's waiting downstairs."

"Reed?"

"Mr. Jablon."

"Whatever for?"

"You, of course."

"Well, I'm not going to talk to him. I will see Angelica if . . ."

"Angelica's in the hospital, under sedation. Perhaps he'll tell you he attacked his daughter-in-law in the art room, exonerating the dogs, and you can call Reed off."

"Well, I've got my seminar now, so I haven't time to hear confessions; besides, he ought to deliver those to the police."

"Stop down and say hello to the old chap. You've really got the wind up, haven't you, Kate?"

"I don't notice you offering your husband as a tethered goat, and you're every bit as worried about the Theban as I am."

"More worried, which is why I would have stuck to

the dog story. My husband's a tethered goat on Madison Avenue, if you really want to know."

Kate looked at Julia a minute. "Sorry," she said. "I'm behaving abominably. One misuses one's friends in the knowledge that they will stand for it. Perhaps we ought to be as considerate of those we love as of those we don't care for at all, but for some reason we never are."

"Thank God for that," Julia said. "Give Mr. Jablon a few kind words, and I will wander in a purposeful way through the corridors, making sure there is no gathering in groups, but a vigorous return to our usual high level of activity. What a hope."

But in fact the school did settle down with great firmness of purpose to its varied tasks. And Kate, hearing the noise on the stairway, was glad that the building was no longer empty.

Mr. Jablon, who rose when he saw her enter the lobby, said much the same thing.

"Please sit down," Kate said, sinking into a chair herself. "I have my seminar now. Do you think Angelica will be back with us soon?"

"I don't know. She doesn't want to come back, which is very bad, of course. Will, that's what is important in these matters, in all matters. Will."

"Perhaps it's not so much a matter of will as of confidence."

"It is a matter of knowing what one should do."

"Is it? I've come to wonder about that. For myself, I've discovered that when I ask myself what I *should* do I always tumble into confusion. The only clear question is to ask oneself what one *wants* to do."

"Isn't that mere self-indulgence?"

"It sounds like it certainly, but oddly enough, it isn't. The 'should' people are really indulging themselves by never really finding out what they want. It has taken me many years to learn that discovering what one wants is the true beginning of a spiritual journey. I suspect you are interested in spiritual journeys."

"Why do you suspect that?"

"Instinct. Recognition, perhaps. Mr. Jablon, almost all the violence and evil in the world come from the 'should' people. I'm ever so certain of that."

"And are your long-haired, bomb-throwing college students who serve the Communist conspiracy 'should' people?" His face became suffused with anger.

"Of course they are. I don't grant they're part of a Communist conspiracy, not believing much in conspiracies anyway—they're too difficult to work out. But those students are as 'should' as you can get, which is one of the reasons they are indistinguishable from the radical right." Kate paused a minute, thinking of Antigone. She must mention to the students—well, perhaps not today—that Antigone had known a deep, undeniable want, to bury the body of her brother. One didn't really have to find religious reasons for her need; it is deeply human to treat dead bodies decently. But Creon had driven them, and primarily himself, to disaster because he was certain that Antigone's brother *should* not be buried.

Mr. Jablon, with an effort, returned to practical matters as, Kate supposed, he had always done when questions tempted him down the primrose path of emotional discourse. "Is everyone satisfied with the explanation of my daughter-in-law's death—that she was frightened into a heart attack by the dogs?" he asked.

"More or less." Kate paused. "As it happens, my husband intends tonight to convince himself at least whether or not the dogs could have failed to notice her and report, so to speak, her presence. If they were so busy frightening her to death, you see, they would hardly have trotted away to set off their signal at the proper time. If they did fail, it would hardly explain why she came here, but perhaps there would be little inclination to investigate that."

"I see. Would you, Mrs. Fansler, be kind enough to let me know the result of tonight's experiment? Of course, if you would rather, I'll speak to Miss Tyringham. . . ."

"It will probably be all right for me to let you know; I will if it is. And *Miss* Fansler is correct."

"Your husband, you said."

"Yes. I must hurry, Mr. Jablon. Thank you." Let him gnaw away at that one, she thought, popping into the elevator. Had Angelica's mother taken the elevator that night, and if so, who had run it for her, and if not . . . Oh, Kate thought, the hell with it.

Kate entered the seminar room prepared, if need be, to jettison the schedule—which called for discussions and reports on Ismene and Haemon—and allow the group, all of whom were now, if they had not for years been, close associates of Angelica's, to discuss her mother's death. One of the principles with which Miss Tyringham had endowed the Theban was the necessity of allowing the structured curriculum to embrace, immediately and upon impulse, any recent event which seemed to relate to it, however tangentially. The school's, all schools' tendencies, had been to say, in effect, That is important, but we must return to the Egyptian dynasty which is the subject matter for today. Miss Tyringham's *vade mecum* for a vital school included the rule that the connections discoverable between the Egyptian dynasties and current problems are the breath of life, for Egypt and education both. Kate, poised therefore on the edge of a heart-to-heart about Mrs. Jablon, found herself confined by the students firmly within the bounds of Ismene's destiny. The members of the seminar had determined either to abide by the advice of the assembly, or to protect Angelica.

Irene Rexton's report amounted to a defense of Ismene's position. She chooses, in the beginning of the play, to preserve rather than risk her life and her safety. She joins the great majority of those who are willing to be unnoticed and insignificant. When, after Antigone's capture, she offers to share Antigone's fate, she is rightly denied martyrdom now, having refused it earlier. It is easy enough, Irene suggested, to sneer at Ismene, but without the Ismenes of the world, what would the Antigones do for a background against which to flaunt their glory?

"You feel she's mainly a foil for Antigone, the way Laertes is for Hamlet?" Freemond asked.

"I guess so," Irene said. "Even if that isn't her intention, it's her destiny. What I'm arguing, though, is that we couldn't possibly have a world of Antigones, but we do have a world of Ismenes, who have all the family problems too, and I think we ought to give them credit."

"The silent majority," Alice said.

"The majority, anyway. Yet with guts, guts to take it,

I mean, as well as dish it out, which is what they are never credited with."

"I don't see," Betsy said, "why the silent majority has suddenly got to be endowed with Ismene's virtues, just because like her they lack guts to take action, to change things."

"Obviously," Freemond said, "Ismene is there to show up Creon, among other reasons. His malevolence toward her, his being so tyrannical toward her, proves that he's not interested in justice, or even law, but in power."

"She shows where his hostility is."

"Yet," Elizabeth said, "when we acted out with, that is, if you think about it, well, his anger there isn't . . ." Her voice trailed off.

"Even Angelica as Creon couldn't work up much anger against Ismene pounding the mattress," Alice said, "so it seems to me . . ." She was silenced by glares.

"Mattress?" Kate asked. "Have I missed something?"

"Alice has a habit of running off at the mouth," Freemond said, "and she's occasionally even known to hallucinate. Who else could imagine Creon and a mattress together?" It had happened, of course, the connection between the Egyptian dynasty and today, but these were seniors, and Kate was too much in the confidence of the Establishment to be shown connections.

"Why do you think Ismene wants to die with Antigone?" Kate asked into the silence.

Freemond undertook to answer. "For much the same reason, eventually, that Antigone chooses to die with her brother: because the reason for continued living has vanished."

"There's nothing remarkable that I can see about Ismene," Betsy said, "she's exactly what one would expect. It is Antigone who amazes one—imagine Sophocles being able to conceive her."

"Ismene's a bore, naturally, being the ordinary woman despite fascinating parents," Alice said. "Haemon's the one with guts; how many men would choose to die with a female martyr? I ask you. The only man who showed any interest in Joan of Arc was some soldier who plucked her heart from the fire, which did her one hell of a lot of good. But Haemon stabbed himself over Antigone's body, and no one, I pray to God, is going to make some big Freudian thing out of *that*."

The class laughed, and turned to Haemon, whom Elizabeth McCarthy found sinful, arrogant, and failing in respect for his parents, to everyone's delight.

"My God," Alice said. "What he, like, absolutely *proves* is that courtesy is wasted on parents. Haemon was sirring his father all over the place, but his father sneered at him just the same. What Haemon was lacking in was respect for himself, until it was too late."

Other words were said, but those echoed in Kate's mind after the seminar was over. She asked Betsy Stark to remain behind to discuss the possible entry of her poem into the school poetry contest.

"If you haven't any immediate commitment," Kate said.

"That's O.K.," Betsy said, dropping her book bag to the floor, and eying Kate warily.

Kate went to the door and closed it. "Sit down, Betsy," she said. "Don't worry, I shan't whip out a gun and hold it to your head. My intentions are frankly dishonorable, but I won't hide them."

"It's not about the poem?"

"That's an excuse, though Mrs. Johnson does want me to urge you to enter it, and Mrs. Copland is anxious for at least one entry from each teacher, so you're like my only opportunity."

Betsy laughed. "I don't care if you enter it, or if I do. But it's a poem that lends itself to misunderstanding, which the discussion here sure demonstrated."

"I know," Kate said. The class had accused Betsy of trying to turn Tiresias's boy into Peter Pan, than which there was, as Kate readily agreed, no more hideous fate. But why, she had asked, must we deprive ourselves of an interesting idea because Barrie appealed to the Victorian fear of sex?

"The truth is," she said now, "I need help about Angelica. I think I might, just possibly might, be able to offer her a hand in crawling out of the abyss, but I don't want to make any ghastly mistakes. Sooo—I'm pumping you, as Angelica says. I'm not asking you to betray any confidences, dearly as I'd love to know what you've been doing with mattresses—involving Creon, that is."

"Why me?" Betsy asked.

"I don't know exactly, but when I came to consider, it seemed obvious."

"That I was likelier to spill?"

"I won't dignify that with an answer; you appear to me more mature, at least in some ways; bright enough, anyway, to figure out that mysteries, particularly those involving the death of one's mother, are always more threatening than the truth."

Kate spoke truthfully about Betsy, but not the entire truth. She could guess something of Betsy, poised on the razor's edge between commitment to her individual destiny and longing for the accepted destiny of a feminine place in a male world. "There is no woman," a misogynist colleague of Kate's at the university had once said to her, "who will not exchange any gift she may have for success with men. Occasionally, very occasionally, you find a woman who has had success with men, and whose gift, when she comes to value it, is still intact." Kate knew well enough the humiliation that society, even so enlightened a society as the Theban, prepares for its unpretty members. "Dogs" they are called by the boys they would like to attract—odd how the idea of dogs kept intruding itself—and they are forced either to attend social occasions on which, like rejected slaves, they are not chosen, or to refuse to attend them, which is an admission of failure of nerve—both demeaning choices. Girls like Betsy, if they could wait without bitterness for the opportunity to meet men, as opposed to boys, or if they could willingly abandon a role as a man's woman, might find a life—but the dangers of resentment and cynicism were perilous, more perilous, Kate thought, than the dangers of stoning which Antigone faced.

"Sorry," Kate said, "I was following my wandering, will-o'-the-wisp mind, and giving you time to think. You can tell me to go to blazes, you know, and sweep from the room."

"What did you want to know?"

"Well, for a start, what was Angelica's mother like? And how did Angelica feel about her?"

"I was afraid you'd ask that. Oh, not because I'm loath to answer; it's always fun in a way to paint a portrait in vitriol, soothing to the nerves to be nasty and deadly accurate all in one fell swoop. It's just that it's difficult to sound as though one isn't being carried away with the passion of one's words. She was a stinker, in short, and if the dogs got rid of her I think they should be given all the sirloin steak they can eat for a month. Can I sweep out now?"

"Of course not. Go on."

"She was afraid of everything, not just airplanes and fast cars and self-service elevators and streets and shut-in places and heights and poisons and contagious diseases, all of which are more or less rational, at least if they occur one at a time, but that robbers would open both locks if she had two and three locks if she had three, that the man who collects tolls on a bridge would try to hold her hand or give her a skin disease, that the sun would give her freckles, that a transfusion from a Negro would turn her black, that—there, I am beginning to sound as though I were exaggerating, which I'm not, but I soon would be, probably."

"She *was* afraid of dogs?"

"Oh, God yes. Apart from biting you, they gave you diseases, and if a dog licked you you would probably get hepatitis, shingles, and African sleeping sickness before nightfall."

"It sounds rather horrible, certainly. Was she fond of Angelica?"

"She was actually one of those women who is jealous of her own daughter, which I know used to happen in Bette Davis movies, but she's the only person I ever knew who actually *was*."

"I take it she thought of herself as a femme fatale."

"The original sex object. If her hair wasn't properly set, colored, teased, and sprayed the very planets would cease in their orbits, or ought to have, out of sympathy. She had a mind so wooly that a prize sheep would have looked bald beside it, and if either of her children ever tried to talk to her about *anything*, she either pretended to have a heart attack or threw a hysterical fit, depending on how much energy she had to spare at the time."

"But she did have a heart condition, you know."

"If you say so."

"Her doctor says so, emphatically. It was reported quite officially to the police, who could tell anyway, from the autopsy."

"Yes. Well, even the boy who cried wolf ended up facing a wolf one day; in fact, that's the whole point of the story, isn't it?"

"It is, I take it, the point of this one."

"I know that she was actually hospitalized once with what Angelica and Patrick used to call her quote unquote heart attack. I think they simply didn't believe it, though I guess it was true."

"Truer, apparently, than the doctors thought it wise to tell her. I mean, if she was capable of being frightened to death, there was no point in frightening her to death by telling her so. She was, one gathers, not one of those people who want to be told the truth."

"Hardly, though I don't think she would have recognized the truth even in its simplest arithmetical form. By which I mean," Betsy added, apparently feeling that this needed amplification, "two plus two always equaled whatever she wanted it to equal. Hell, she was a fright and no mistake. We all have problems with our mothers, of course," Betsy said, as though she were confirming that they all had two arms and two legs, "but Angelica's mother didn't even achieve a modicum of consistency. She'd say Angelica could have friends overnight and then throw a tantrum in front of them. Oh, I don't know; but the worst was, she tried her best to divide Angelica from her brother and her grandfather; it's to their credit, I think, that she—the mother, that is—never succeeded."

"They all lived with their grandfather, didn't they?"

"Yes. He insisted on it, and reactionary and old fogeyish as he is, and he *is*, I think he was right. He couldn't possibly have gotten custody of the kids when their father died, and he knew it would be fatal to leave them to her tender mercies, so he persuaded her to live with him, bribing her with plenty of money for shoes made out of alligator and coats made out of seal, which would have broken Angelica's heart if everything else had not already broken it—she's a conservationist, of course. He did at least see that they went to good schools, and lived a decent sort of life—actually, it worked out rather well until this damn war. I think, without wholly understanding it when she was young, Angelica knew that her grandfather was doing the right thing, and he had the sense never to speak against her mother, so Angelica didn't have any conflict of loyalties as people always do when they're young about their mothers. Of course, once the old man turned his back on the two of them, the sh—um, there was trouble."

"I've talked to the grandfather, so I understand a little about that. I mention it because I don't want to appear to be pumping you without telling you what I know."

"For someone of your generation you try to be honest, though all of us agree you can't possibly be as straight as you obviously are."

Kate laughed. "What I didn't have the nerve to ask Mr. Jablon," she went on, "is why he was so eager for his grandson to be in a war when his father, Mr. Jablon's son, had died in one."

"Angelica doesn't believe her father died in the war. She thinks he killed himself."

"My dear girl, surely it's a matter of record."

"You sound like Miss Tyringham. It's on the record O.K. He inveigled his way out to Korea and shot himself or something cleverly enough to win the purple heart or the chartreuse kidney or whatever they give you for being wounded in the service of the military, particularly since the fighting had already stopped when he got there, and it wasn't the service of the military that interested him, it was getting away from his horrible wife and dominating father."

"In my opinion, they would never have had wars throughout history if men had not needed an excuse to get away from their wives."

"Do you really? I thought you liked women."

"Certainly I do. But I don't think making them dependent on one man for everything increases their attractions for him; it only increases his guilt if he leaves her, but war takes care of *that*."

"Do you believe in group marriage?"

"Believe in it? I don't even know what it is."

"Well, lots of people live together and change partners, as Fred Astaire used to sing in the dear, dead days."

"You really must meet my husband," Kate said, if he survives, she added privately. "That sounds rather problematic, as though one were a pride of lions without the necessity of working together to catch gazelles. I believe in voluntary associations, but I certainly believe that every woman should contribute to the family kitty by having a job and bringing home part of the bacon. Does that throw any light on my straightness?"

"Do you think you can have comedies of manners about sex if you don't have any ritual about it—courtship, and all that crap?"

"Well, you couldn't have fewer than you have now, so it's worth trying. I'll tell you about sex if you'll tell me about mattresses, and if that sounds like an indecent proposition, it is, since only you can tell me about mattresses, and anyone, including yourself in a few years, can tell you about sex."

"People who are honest are more dishonest than liars because they disarm you. Somerset Maugham said you could make a character sound breathtakingly brilliant by just letting her tell the truth. You ever heard of Esalen?"

"That place in California that cures drug addiction?"

"That's Synanon. Esalen has lots of techniques and we, that is—well, some of us tried this. You hit a mattress, which is soft and doesn't mind taking a beating, and pretend it's whomever you feel hostile toward. That way, you work out the hostility and even recognize some you hadn't wanted to think about, which is always useful. Do you think there shouldn't be any sexual mores at all?"

"Wait a minute. Where did you find out about Esalen—has one of you been there?"

"You can read about it."

"I think women should be virgins when they marry, because their jewel is the most precious thing they have, and how else could they wear white at their wedding when they are handed from one man who owns them to another? You learned it from Mrs. Banister, didn't you?"

"If you know, why are you asking me?" Betsy said, sounding more like a petulant child than she had all afternoon.

"I didn't know until a few minutes ago. It sounds a damn good idea—the mattress bit, I mean. Why be so secretive about it?"

"Well, it wasn't *exactly* what the Theban had in mind under the heading of dramatics. We talk to pillows, too, as though they are our other self with whom we are arguing, or someone else who—people used to kid about our encounter groups, but they never really thought . . ."

"Yes."

"Well, sometimes we had sessions after school, and Mrs. Banister, though she never said so, wasn't certain, anyway we weren't certain . . ."

"If the school would officially approve."

"That's it. Actually, she helped us an awful lot. You can't imagine."

"I think I can, you know. I told Mr. Jablon just today that what one wanted to do was more to the point than what one should do, and you don't know what you want till you face what you hate, face it, and recognize it into proportion."

"In case you're wondering, Mrs. Banister hasn't got any sort of thing over girls, you know what I mean?"

"Perfectly."

"One has to be careful; it's a nasty and suspicious world, though we try not to be more paranoiac than absolutely necessary. I wish I could think of a perfectly sizzling question to ask you about sex . . ."

"When you do, I shall answer it between my blushes."

"I'll remember that. Don't tell . . ."

"Only if necessary, and then only in perfect confidence. Trust me."

"I've decided to," Betsy said, sweeping from the room at last.

Reed didn't sweep into the room; he tiptoed in and cast glances about him with all the furtiveness of an eavesdropper in a Restoration comedy. He carried with him a heavily padded jacket which Mr. O'Hara had insisted upon his wearing against the possibility that the dogs' teeth might close around an arm or neck. While the dogs were guaranteed not to bite or play unnecessarily roughly, precautions were nonetheless taken against their doing any such thing.

The question was, could he find a place where the dogs would overlook him? That was O'Hara's challenge. While doubting that he could, Reed was prepared to try.

The room he had chosen was a small gymnasium, designed for gymnast feats, and hung with ropes, rings, and swinging booms. With agility, Reed swung his lean form up onto the ropes and reached over to the ladderlike rungs which lined the wall. Here, holding on first with one hand and then the other, he donned the jacket. The gymnasium clock, coy behind its protective wire, told him it was three minutes of eight. At eight promptly, O'Hara would release the dogs from the roof. In fact, their departure was announced, so to speak, by the bell which sounded on every hour throughout the school building. With the sound of the bell he swung himself off and hung suspended by the rings from the ceiling like—when Kate had described him she had no idea how literal a description it would be—a tethered goat; well, hamstrung, rather.

He was on a high floor, so the dogs would not be long. Indeed, before long he thought he heard them, their nails clicking on the floor as they emerged, he assumed, listening, from the stairway to begin their methodical survey of all the rooms on the floor.

Although he heard them approaching, heard, because he was listening for it, the sound of their feet and their breath, they were aware of him almost sooner. He was at the farthest corner of the room and high up, but they knew immediately that he was there. The growls began in their throats, and the lips pulled back, baring the teeth. Yes, Reed thought, it's enough to scare anyone to death, enough certainly to frighten a young man into backing up, tripping, and hitting his head, but will they actually let me descend unharmed?

They did not, as he had thought they would, leap for him as he hung in the air. They stood and watched. Slowly, he released his feet and swung himself back over to the ladder on the wall. Their growls increased as he descended, but they did not move. "They won't go for your legs," O'Hara had said. "If you don't try anything cute, they won't touch you. But they are trained to leap for a hand holding a weapon" (hence the jacket, should the dogs hallucinate a weapon where there was none) "and, should you attack them in any other way, they will hurl their weight against your chest and knock you down. But only if you lunge at them."

Lily and Rose, Reed thought, what singularly inappropriate names. He kept his eyes warily upon them as he climbed slowly down. The growls increased, the teeth glared more menacingly, but the dogs did not move. "Get your back against a wall and stay still till I come," O'Hara had said. Reed flirted with the idea of lighting a cigarette and abandoned it. It would calm his nerves, but would it do the same for the nerves of Lily and Rose? He doubted it, Furthermore, the actions necessary to reach beneath the padded jacket for cigarette and lighter seemed unlikely to inspire confidence. Without moving his head, Reed raised his eyes to the gymnasium clock. Even as he did so, O'Hara appeared in the doorway.

"All right, my beauties," he said. And, going forward, he clipped short, stout leashes onto the collars of the dogs. "Glad you picked a high floor," he said to Reed. "I couldn't have done with a much longer wait."

"Nor I," Reed admitted. "O.K. to take the jacket off now?"

O'Hara nodded. "Convinced?" he asked.

"Oh, yes," Reed said. "A very commendable performance. I recommend it to anyone who wants to lose weight fast."

"Did you feel afraid, then?" O'Hara asked.

"Oh, yes," Reed said. "Scared to death, to coin a phrase." And he reached for a cigarette and lit it, breaking, he supposed, one of the school's most stringent rules. Well, he had earned the right.

"Could you," Reed asked, "hold on to those charming ladies while I poke around a bit downstairs? There's something I'm looking for."

"How long will you be?" O'Hara grudgingly asked. He owed Reed a good deal, he knew, for demonstrating both that the dogs were unlikely to have frightened Mrs. Jablon to death and then deserted her, and that they did not viciously attack anyone they found— which nasty suspicion had been voiced more than once since knowledge of the dogs had become general. Still, he didn't care to break the dogs' routine. "I'll take them back to the roof. Call me from the switchboard on the main floor when you're ready to leave; I'll give you ten minutes after that."

"Right. Mr. O'Hara, let me try your patience a minute longer. On the evening Mrs. Jablon was found here . . ."

"The evening before the morning she was found here."

"All right. On the evening of the meeting. You took the parents up in one of the elevators. Was the other elevator on the roof?"

"Yes. I told you that . . ."

"Be patient. No one could have brought that second elevator down without your knowing?"

"Impossible."

"Why?"

"It was up in the auditorium, as high as the elevators go. You would have had to walk all the way, know where to find the key to open the elevator door up there, and bring it down."

"Did you use the other elevator—the one not on the top—to bring the parents and teachers down again?"

"Sure. Ten-fifteen prompt I was up there waiting for them. That's the orders from Miss Tyringham."

"Suppose someone had wanted to leave early?"

"They could have walked down, or rung the elevator bell."

"Were you sitting in the elevator?"

"I was around."

"What does around mean? You were always in the building, always on the first floor?"

"Or just outside the front door. There were a couple of chauffeurs waiting for the parents and I talked to them some. My job is to watch the entrance, not to serve as butler."

"Do the chauffeurs who bring parents wait for them?"

"Sometimes. Mostly, they go off for a while, with orders to be back at ten. They usually get back sooner and stand around."

"O.K.," Reed said. "Thanks. Do you happen to know which parents come with chauffeurs? If not, I can get the information from Miss Tyringham, I suppose; the chauffeurs might have seen something."

O'Hara knew the chauffeurs by sight, and their cars, of course, but that was all. "I'll give you ten minutes after you call," he said, turning toward the stairs with Lily and Rose.

"By the way," Reed said, "if the dogs heard someone downstairs, would they break their routine and go see?"

"Of course. They'd find the person wherever he was. I'd miss a regular alarm, and go to look for them; it might take a little longer." He disappeared up the stairway.

Reed ran the many flights down to the lobby, stopping on the way to crush out his cigarette and drop the stub in his pocket. He switched the lights on in the lobby and looked around. The entrance, which was large, rather like a theater entrance, had a double set of doors, which formed two sides of the entrance hall leading to the lobby. He saw what he was looking for immediately, behind a set of glass doors in the entrance hall; the doors led to an emergency stairway from the floor below. Lighting another cigarette, he went to phone O'Hara.

"What's the dolly for?" Reed asked when O'Hara had answered. "The one off the entrance hall under a canvas?"

"To move supplies. Papers, books, anything. After they've been delivered."

"O.K.," Reed said. "I'm off. With one last question." And he asked it.

He called Kate from a phone booth on the corner to tell her he had emerged unscathed from the lions' den. They were very well-trained lions. "I know now what happened at the school," he said. "But I don't know what happened before, or how she got there. Rose and Lily send you their love, or so I discerned. O'Hara obviously wasn't thinking of you at all, but I made up for that by thinking of you all the time. Did you really, in your ferociously upper-class girlhood, hang from those rings for fun?"

Ten

ARLY on the following day, for which no seminar was scheduled, Kate awoke with the uneasy conviction that she had determined upon some action and the inability to remember exactly what it was. I shall probably emerge from this entire Theban episode, she unhappily thought, no longer able to sleep in the mornings. I shall have to join Reed in the shower and learn all of Cole Porter's lyrics. She mentioned this dismal conclusion to Reed, who had just arisen. "Excellent," he said, and disappeared into the bathroom, whence, shortly, could be heard the strains of *Kiss Me, Kate*.

Kate gathered her wits together sufficiently, first, to remember what she had decided to do, and then, which was harder, to decide how to do it. The day seemed, the more she thought about it, to contain an amazingly large number of conversations, heart-to-heart talks, or what she hoped would be heart-to-heart talks, and just

155

plain worming round. She began upon this rather long series of investigations by calling Miss Tyringham at school. Miss Tyringham, as Kate had learned, arrived at the Theban shortly before eight every morning, and could be reached in her office by those to whom she was willing to speak after they had identified themselves to Miss Strikeland at the switchboard, whose arrival was planned to precede Miss Tyringham's by a matter of minutes. Miss Strikeland had failed to arrive, despite the threats of weather, strikes, and power failures, once only, when the crosstown bus she was on had broken down in such a way that the driver was unable to open the doors. Miss Tyringham had been so worried by this uncharacteristic tardiness that she became visibly distraught and sat there working the switchboard herself in the hope of some news. This morning, however, Miss Strikeland was in place and soon put Kate through.

"How are you?" came Miss Tyringham's cheerful voice. "I understand your gallant husband faced our menacing beasts with commendable sang-froid. Mr. O'Hara is beside himself with admiration, feeling that total canine vindication has been accomplished. Where does that leave us with our other problems?"

"I'm not sure," Kate said, "but I'm full of theories, and shall certainly never get a moment's rest until I test them. For that I need your permission or at least acquiescence."

"Why don't you stop in this morning as soon as you can? I shall have to cut two meetings, but it's all in a day's work. How much time do you need?"

"Oh, well, probably not too long. Sorry to barge in on the school day, but of course I've become compulsive and insist on bringing this whole business to some conclusion. I knew that the *Antigone* seminar would interfere to some extent with my work on the Victorians, but not that I would become so feverish. Reed says the only way to get rid of temptation is to give in to it; I hope he's right."

"You're suggesting he may have been right when he counseled us to abandon the whole investigation?"

"Well, he was certainly right about not stopping halfway through. Nine o'clock then?" Kate rang off.

She decided to walk to the Theban, since she had ample time, taxis were impossible to get at that hour of the morning, the buses were crowded, and walking would help to clear her head. In fact, she wanted to reduce her confused emotions to some sort of order. She had not many doubts, after talking to Reed last night, about what had happened on the night before the morning when the body so mysteriously appeared at the Theban. There were a great many details to be worked out, of course, either laboriously or more quickly, through a lucky chance. Discovering hidden events is like searching for a misplaced document immediately required. You may hit on it the first place you look, or you may have to peer into every cranny and file folder you own, but if the document is there you will find it, and it will all come to the same thing in the end.

What troubled Kate was whether or not the Theban or the Jablons would emerge from this investigation healthier than if it had never been undertaken. Indeed, could any institution or family or relationship survive the pressures of these difficult times? She remembered how, in earlier years, one returned to the educational institutions from which one had graduated only occasionally, but then in the certainty of finding peace. One had always thought to oneself, If only I could come back here where everything is ordered and in proportion. But what such places were there now? Whatever had brought this body to the Theban, or the boy to the Theban before it, had shattered forever the mirage of the school as a place of peace. Dogs patrolled its rooms, and the dead and frightened were found upon its premises.

The Theban stood on one of those delicious side streets on the East Side which appear unchanged from earlier, more halcyon times. This is an illusion—since the town houses were almost all divided into apartments, or even into offices. The street was quiet, nonetheless, tree-lined and airy; there were no tall buildings in the immediate vicinity, the Theban itself, ten stories high, being the tallest. Was it a street on which anyone was likely to notice very much? Its busiest moment came in the afternoon, when the buses gathered to drive the younger students home. Only then did the demure, if institutional-looking building declare itself a school. For, like all elegant girls' schools in New York, it bore no name, no sign, no plaque upon its entrance to announce itself. One either knew this was the Theban, or one had no business knowing.

Miss Tyringham greeted Kate with a kind of fatigued relief.

"You are all right, aren't you?" Kate asked. "I've got so used to seeing people in positions of authority in academia grow tired, ill, and full of despair and foreboding that perhaps I've become unduly alarmed. But you do look what the English call nervy."

"Oh, it's just one of those flu things I always seem to get at winter's last gasp, nothing serious, what my mother used to call up-doings and down-doings. At least," she added, "that does for an explanation. In fact, of course, I'm worried."

"About the body?"

"Among much else. We don't talk frankly about it, you know, but we're running into a good bit of trouble—we, in that sentence, being the figures of authority at private schools. Oh, I don't just mean pants, and Moratorium Days, or even the threat of drugs. A number of our girls don't go to school at all, particularly the seniors. I think if the figure of how many middle- and upper-class youngsters in New York were simply not attending school at this moment were published— which heaven forbid—the Mr. Jablons would really begin to fret."

"Is Angelica's staying out part of all that, do you think?"

"Possibly, possibly not. She certainly had a hard time. She's home now, but doesn't want to consider school."

"One of the things I wanted to ask you is if you have any objection to my going to see her. Of course, I'll courteously ask her grandfather, but he's hardly likely to refuse unless Angelica does. Do you mind if I talk to him too?"

"No, I think not. We've got to get to the bottom of this, if that's possible in anything under a fifteen-year psychoanalysis."

"Long private analysis is going out of style, I think. The new thing's encounter groups, acting out and all that."

"Is it, indeed? Well, to be frank, I never could muster up much faith in psychoanalysis, though we've had an extraordinary number of our students in therapy if not analysis over the years. There was a time when it seemed as de rigueur as orthodonture, and that, I've always suspected, was necessary in twenty percent of the cases, at a generous estimate."

"Have you heard anything of encounter groups here?"

"Here at the Theban? No." She looked at Kate. "Oh, dear," she said, "you're trying to tell me something, or if you're not trying, I'm hearing it anyway. Never mind, I don't want to know. I was right anyway about the *Antigone*, wasn't I? Isn't it still relevant?"

"I'm beginning to think extraordinarily so. For example, when Creon finally becomes convinced that he was wrong not to have buried Polynices and to have punished Antigone for doing so, he goes to release her from the cave where he's had her interred. But he stops on the way to bury Polynices, and when he gets to the cave it's too late. She's dead, and so is everyone he cared for. Oh, don't look so stricken, I'm not predicting any more bodies, merely suggesting that perhaps it is Angelica who should get our first attention—doubtless just a fancy, to bring my subject into the news, a common academic ploy."

"Oh, dear. Go ahead and cope with the Jablons if you will be so good. What else have you on your agenda?"

"More dreary questions. Tell me a bit, in a rapid sort

of way, about the five other girls in the seminar. You advise the seniors, don't you; consult about college, and all that?"

"Oh, yes. I also hold a class in ethics, a Theban tradition, if you can believe it—but of course you must remember."

"Certainly I do. What in God's name does ethics mean these days?"

"Well may you ask. I've ended up doing what everyone in the academic world does do now, I let the girls decide what they want to discuss, hoping to heaven it isn't sex, because of course, no matter what people say, that really can't be handled by the school except scientifically and in a factual sort of way—our science teachers take turns at it, with a frankness that astounds me. But my unmarried state happily protected me from the fate of discussing sex—they were afraid of startling me, I suppose. What they did want to discuss was their parents, which was almost worse than sex. However, I managed to turn *that* into a more or less organized combination of questionnaire and sociological study. We asked all the students in the last two years of the upper school what they most objected to in the behavior of their parents and then—this was where I thought I was rather clever—we asked the parents of the two first years in the upper school (because we didn't want people actually comparing notes) what they most objected to in the behavior of their children. It all turned out to be fascinating, and if we want to call it ethics, who's to stop us? Which seems a remarkably long-winded way of saying, yes, I do know something about the seniors."

"Did all the parents and all the students agree, more

or less, on what they couldn't stand in the other group?" Kate asked, fascinated.

"Oh, yes, it was really quite unanimous. The students objected to the fact that their parents were dishonest and pressuring about their values. That is, they might *say* they wouldn't put pressure on the girl to get good marks and go to a good college, but it was perfectly clear to the girls that that's just what the parents were doing. They *said* they didn't care about material things, but did, and so forth. The girl's hairdo mattered more than her ideas. Hypocrisy, in a word. The parents, on the other hand, objected that they could never do anything right. That no matter how they tried to get on with their adolescent children, and meet them halfway, everything, *everything* they did was always wrong, even if they did exactly opposite things on two days running. The discussion cleared the air, and we all concluded that, while parents could stand corrected, children were bound to find their parents lacking, and there was nothing for it but to bear parenthood with what fortitude God gives."

"Or avoid it."

"Well, rather late in the day for that in the case of Theban parents. Being a parent *is* rather harder these days; there are so many more things to say 'no' to where the society isn't helping you at all, and the dangers, such as drugs, syphilis, and car accidents and rapes are even more frightening than ever they were. So much for ethics. What else do you want to know?"

"Just give me a bit about the family backgrounds, where they live, values, all that."

"Freemond Oliver is absolutely top drawer, though if you quote me I shall deny ever having used the phrase.

We've had four Olivers at the Theban, and there are a couple of boys besides. They live in a duplex on lower Park Avenue and Freemond . . ."

"O.K. Betsy Stark I know best of the girls, but not what sort of family she comes from."

"I take it money is what you want to hear about."

"Not to put too fine a point on it, yes; that and any indications of excessive, or excessively limited, freedom."

"The Starks have money from the mother's side of the family. The grandmother pays for the children's education. The family lives on East Seventy-something, I forget just where, one of those big, spacious, prewar apartments which went co-op."

"And the mother is homely but vivacious and bright, and she thinks her husband married her for her money, and so does Betsy."

"You seem to know more about them than I do."

"I don't know anything. I'm surmising and I'm probably wrong. Isn't it funny how people with money are never certain they're loved for themselves, but people with beauty are always sure of it?"

"That's either very profound or doesn't make any sense at all."

"Like most of my remarks. And Alice Kirkland?"

"Ah, a problem that one. It's always so annoying when rebelliousness takes the form of pure rudeness. The youngest of the family, and at home with parents who indulge her ridiculously, not even requiring the bare modicum of courtesy. We recommended boarding school *very* strongly, but Alice wasn't having any. Of course, we never insist. Money. Oh, lots. Mr. Kirkland recently gave us a check for fifty thousand dollars. He

163

said he had made it in a phone call that took thirty seconds, and he was anxious not to be a philistine."

"Did you take it?"

"Naturally, my dear, though not without pointing to the story of the plumber who charged fifty dollars and fifty cents for fixing the furnace: fifty cents for tapping, and fifty dollars for knowing where to tap. Who else have you got?"

"Elizabeth McCarthy and Irene Rexton."

"Ah, yes. Elizabeth was at school with the Mesdames, of course, until this year. We don't usually take girls for the last year, but her school recommendations were impeccable, and she came with letters not only from three sets of Theban parents, but from the Cardinal himself."

"I see. And Irene? Lovely to look at, delightful to know, as Reed would say."

"And heaven to kiss, I'm sure all the men would agree. She's the adopted child of a pair of Columbia anthropologists—both dark as the natives they are always wandering off to live among, and with views toward adolescent independence that would do credit to the Samoans. She was the only student with no complaints to make about her parents."

"She's such a shatteringly conventional child, always defending Ismene and simple womanhood."

"I know. The bringing-up of children is a total enigma. Though perhaps if one looks like that, one must be conventional or die."

"They live around Columbia, I suppose?"

"Yes, I think so, let me check." Miss Tyringham leafed through a loose-leaf notebook. "Here we are,

Morningside Drive. That's the lot, including the Jablons, whom I gather you know all about."

"Or will do my best to find out about."

"You must tell me someday what all this is in aid of."

"I promise to tell you, even if it turns out, as it probably will, not to be in aid of anything. I'll just jot down the addresses, and ask one more question, though a sticky one. No, I've two more. Do you mind if Mr. Jablon knows that Reed discovered the dogs unlikely to have missed Miss Jablon, had she been there? He's mighty anxious for the information, and I'd like to find out why."

"I can't see why he shouldn't know. At the moment I've adopted the policy of straightforwardness, which causes a lot less trouble in the end and anyhow comes to me naturally."

"Well, try to be straightforward about this. Suppose one of the faculty at the Theban, or one of the parents, was in any way involved with Mrs. Jablon's death and presence here—I don't mean killed her, of course; she wasn't killed, as you know. Would you be inclined to be tolerant about it?"

"It would depend. No, I'm not fudging, it would. A parent is hardly my business. A teacher is. The whole question would be whether in the light of this new information I still considered her able to do her work properly."

"Which is not very straightforward."

"No it's not. But then, neither is your question. You're asking me whether or not you are free to tell me the name of a teacher who is involved, since if I am likely to fire her, you are not free. It is only possible to find straightforward answers to straightforward questions, if then."

"Fair enough. Anyway, it's only the merest suspicion, so don't worry about it. I'm also wondering if I should stop right here, but somehow I know I mustn't. Not if we want to get to the cave in time."

"The cave?"

"Where Angelica is. The cave of guilt, perhaps."

"Oh dear, oh dear."

"I'm also interested in Grandpa, oddly enough. And in the Theban. Will you keep on the dogs regardless?"

"Oh, yes. They're still the cheapest and best protection we could have, and now that they're so famous, they'll be even better. *And* since their infallibility has been so decisively proved."

"I wonder, though, at your hiring such a misogynist to protect a girls' school."

"My dear, it is always those who fear women who are most assiduous to protect them for their own good, provided of course they aren't sexual maniacs, and Mr. O'Hara is not only past it, he comes with the best recommendations from the Pentagon on down."

"Guaranteed above reproach."

"And beneath contempt, you suggest. He's an excellent watchman all the same. I'm old enough to prefer that to his agreeing to every opinion I hold. Rose and Lily, fortunately, have no opinions whatever."

"Are you answering my sticky question? Yes, oh dear, I see that you are," Kate said, and came away.

She stopped in the lobby and imposed upon Miss Strikeland long enough to call Mr. Jablon. Kate was aware that Reed had managed to call her on the previous evening from a nearby phone booth, but not even this knowledge could alter her conviction that no telephone in New York City was in operating condition. Usually their receivers hung straight down in a forlorn state of impotence—if one was lucky, that is. Otherwise, one dropped dimes in to be rewarded neither by a dial tone nor the return of one's money. Like most people who continue not only to survive in New York but to love the city, Kate had learned to avoid the most obvious sources of frustration and anger: taxis at rush hour, phone booths at any time. Miss Strikeland connected her with commendable efficiency.

But Mr. Jablon was not at home; he had already left for the office. Kate was surprised to discover that an elderly man who could devote days to observing school lobbies should have an office, but she asked for and was given the telephone number and succeeded, with more help from Miss Strikeland, in reaching Mr. Jablon there. He said he would be glad to see her in his office as soon as she could get there. With a wave of thanks to Miss Strikeland, Kate continued what was clearly going to be an exceedingly peripatetic day.

Mr. Jablon's office turned out to be in a new and elegant building on Park Avenue in the fifties. He occupied a large office with a small entrance hall, the door to which he opened for Kate himself. He had fixed up his office as a rather comfortable living room, and Kate sat in one comfortable chair while he sat in another. Against one wall stood a large desk.

"I do *some* work there," Mr. Jablon said, following her glance; "investments and so forth. I call my broker, he calls me. I read various stock-market sheets, the *Wall Street Journal*, and the *National Observer*. I could do all that at home, but this is a place to leave home and come to. It gives a shape to the day."

Kate nodded. Before she had been asked to take the class at the Theban, she had coped, as all who work at home must cope, with a day not given a shape by the necessity of leaving for work at a specified time, and then returning. It was the old question of freedom and time flapping about one. Unless one structured the day very carefully, and observed schedules with a rigidity which would have done credit to a Trappis monastery, one wasted time and time wasted one.

"You wanted to know the result of last night's experiment with the dogs," Kate said, "and Miss Tyringham has given me permission to tell you. The dogs immediately discovered Reed, who made some half-hearted attempts to conceal himself from them. He is convinced no one could hide in the building and remain undetected by the dogs."

"I see," Mr. Jablon said. "Then I will have to change my story."

"I rather thought you might," Kate said. "What was it going to be—that you had persuaded your daughter-in-law to come with you to the school, that you had lost track of her there and had gone home leaving her to be frightened by the dogs?"

"Something like that. I was afraid, you see, that one of the children . . . but as it happened, the police suspected me of something, and they looked into my activities and discovered I had an alibi for the entire evening. I hope I am unique in trying to conceal the fact that I *wasn't* on the scene of the crime, but nothing is new under the sun, is it?"

"Where were you?" Kate asked. "I hope you don't mind my forthright questions. I'm willing to attempt more circumlocutions if you prefer."

"I do as a rule," Mr. Jablon admitted. "I like the social amenities, which oil the wheels of progress. But, under the circumstances, I concede the need for shortcuts. I was home for dinner, with Angelica, a friend of hers from school named Freemond Oliver, my grandson Patrick, and my daughter-in-law."

"Does Angelica often have friends for dinner?"

"Lately she does. I discovered, not too long ago, that my daughter-in-law was discouraging this by claiming it made too great claims on her time and energy, but I pointed out that the servants were quite able to undertake any additional work, and that I thought children should have a home to which they could bring their friends. The truth of the matter is, however, that Angelica has only recently brought her friends, because she was ashamed of her home."

"Ashamed of it? I was under the impression . . ."

"Not of the physical home, which is perfectly acceptable, but of her mother and me. Her mother was as likely as not, I'm afraid, to have some sort of hysterical scene, or embarrass Angelica in some way by some tactless remark, and she was ashamed of me because of my opinions, which she called conservative as though that word were an insult; I look upon it as a compliment. I try to conserve."

"I see," Kate said. She felt inclined to credit Mrs. Banister and the encounter groups for Freemond's presence. If you have shrieked out your hostilities and angers, and your friends know all about your mother and grandfather, there is no longer any point in concealing your home from them. Indeed, they, as impartial observers, can confirm your right to resentment.

"After dinner," he continued, "everyone disappeared, as they always do, and I went to my bridge club. I arrived there at nine, and returned home shortly before one. I was playing bridge the entire time. It is a private bridge club, men only; rubber bridge, not duplicate."

Kate thought of various detective stories she had long ago read in which the murderer had used bridge as an alibi. But careful questioning by the detective had revealed that, while dummy, the suspect had managed to race to wherever it was, kill whoever it was, and reappear in time for the new deal. It seemed unlikely here.

"I was never out of sight of someone while there," Mr. Jablon offered, dispensing with the bridge-playing murderer of Kate's fancy. "I always stay around to see how a hand's going to come out. And once it's over we discuss it."

"Was everyone in when you got home?"

"I certainly assumed so. In fact, as I now know, they were, except for my daughter-in-law. Angelica became hysterical on the following morning when the news of her mother's death was received. I called the family physician, who told me candidly that she ought to be removed to a hospital, since he felt she was in danger of doing harm to herself. He also recommended psychiatric help, but this Angelica adamantly refused, so we did not insist. The one thing everyone seems to agree to about psychiatric help is that it does no good if the patient does not desire it."

"What about your grandson?"

"Patrick has been in a strange and difficult mood for months; the experience with the dogs at the school did not help this. In his position, despising me for my despising him, I would have cleared out altogether and made my own way. That, however, does not seem the habit of today's youth. They are perfectly willing to accept shelter and clothing and food from someone whom they consider little better than a criminal."

"Surely he never actually called you a criminal?"

"He did, many times. For example, his discovery—that is, he asked me and I told him—that I owned stock in companies which made war materials gave him, in his opinion, the right to suspect my entire system of values. I pointed out that he had been educated and was now being fed by those same stocks, but that only added guilt to insurrection."

"Don't you feel he had a point at all?"

"No. I will not, for example, own stock in tobacco companies which manufacture cigarettes. I consider their advertising immoral, and the dangers of smoking more than adequately proved. Certainly I wouldn't own stock in any company that trafficked in addictive drugs if any such were offered on the market. Patrick's particular complaint was about Dow Chemical. He pleaded with me to sell the stock, since they made napalm, a burning jelly which is dropped on human beings and burns away their skin; it cannot be wiped off. Patrick could not understand how anyone could agree to make such a thing. He also discovered that we use Saran Wrap and various other Dow products and threw them out."

"But you didn't sell the stock."

"I made up my mind to. After all, I object to some

companies for reasons which may be as arbitrary. But just as I was about to sell the stock, Dow lost the government contract for napalm and Patrick agreed there was no longer any reason to sell, since Dow was no more militaristic than many other stocks in my portfolio."

"But at least you had agreed to something. . . ."

"I was sorry later that I had. Not only was there a wrong principle involved, but I support this country's so-called military-industrial complex. Nothing about war is pretty, or humane. It is only necessary."

Kate found herself troubled in Mr. Jablon's presence. She did not agree with him, that went without saying and she felt no special impulse to say it. She was too familiar with his attitudes to waste time upon them when other matters were more pressing. What troubled her was that she rather liked Mr. Jablon, whose personal judgments she suspected of being on the whole honorable and defensible. Like many of his generation and his experience, he had lost the connection between his personal morality and the national morality of his beloved country, on whose behalf he was willing to defend offensive practices on the grounds of national necessity that he would never for a moment have endorsed as personal actions. As Matthew Arnold had perceived a century earlier, the double standard had horribly damaged the quality of national life, robbing it of sweetness and light.

"What do you think happened to your daughter-in-law, Mr. Jablon?"

"I don't know. I accept the word of the police doctors and of her private physician that she was killed by a shock which brought on a heart attack. She had heart trouble, though none of us took it seriously enough, I'm afraid. On the other hand, I read recently of a four-year-old child who died of fright in the dentist's chair—too much adrenalin poured into her heart. I don't know what frightened my daughter-in-law."

"Did the police say she was necessarily frightened, or was that just assumed because of the dogs?"

"I don't think they said 'frightened,' no. Her doctor said it might have been a frenzy. She was given, that is, inclined toward frenzies."

The understatement of the month, probably, Kate thought. She did not push Mr. Jablon on the point, admiring his discretion.

"I am interested," she said, "in discovering what did actually happen that night, and who is responsible for your daughter-in-law's death. I'd like, in pursuit of the truth, to go to your home and talk to your grandson and granddaughter, if they are willing. Have you any objection?"

"To your going to my home? No. Nor to your questioning my servants, if you find that necessary. I trust you to confine yourself to what is strictly essential. But I haven't much hope of your finding out what happened, and I think you are deluding yourself if you have hope. As to my grandchildren, they are perfectly capable of telling you to go to blazes."

"Do you intend to take any action against the school?"

"Because of my daughter-in-law? Certainly not. What would be the purpose of that?"

"They might be accused of negligence."

"I doubt it. You apparently have plenty of people to testify that the dogs would not have frightened her and left."

"One can always get people to testify to anything, perfectly sincerely I mean. Nothing is certain. And it might be presumed that her body's being found there was sufficient evidence of negligence."

"Are you trying to persuade me to sue?"

"Certainly not. But I don't know what I may discover. Miss Tyringham has, with extraordinary honor and courage, it seems to me, opted for the truth, if it is discoverable. I happen to think seeking the truth is also the intelligent plan to pursue, but naturally I would. We can't know what we may discover, and I want to be certain that you do not suppose me to be suggesting collusion."

"I see. Well, there is no benefit I can discover in suing the school. Not even in suing it for the radical ideas it has inculcated into my granddaughter. After all, I was always free to remove her. You're suggesting that once you set foot on a road such as this you must follow it to the end, without knowing, before you get there, what the end will be. I understand that. To be frank, if I could have convinced everyone and ended the whole affair with the story of how I had been responsible for my daughter-in-law's presence in the school, I would have been pleased. But, if that is not possible, one must accept the necessary revelations."

"This question is none of my business," Kate said, "but if Patrick had been drafted and gone into the army, would you have taken any steps to keep him away from the fighting in Vietnam?"

"I would have, certainly, using what contacts and influence I had."

"And that doesn't strike you as wrong, the way Patrick's defection strikes you as wrong?"

"Not in the least. What contacts and influence I have I have earned. And, if they had not been sufficient, Patrick would have had to go. I would never have interfered with his country's decision about him." Kate shook her head. "Miss Fansler, the police questioned the man who for forty years has made my shirts and sold me my ties. As soon as they left him, he called me up to tell me so. His desire to warn me was based on long knowledge of me and my reputation."

"That's quite different, I think. One is a network of personal devotion, which I defend. The other is a network of influence, which I deplore. Oh, I know, we all use influence. But your shirt man did not lie to the police."

"Of course not."

"But, if your grandson failed to go to Vietnam, someone with less influence would have gone in his place."

"I realize that. That is the way of the world, and it doesn't do to pretend the world is not a jungle."

"Well," Kate said rising, "we haven't time to argue it now. I don't believe you believe all you're saying. I don't believe you would manufacture napalm. Or am I wrong? You would manufacture it, but you would not personally drop it on babies."

"One has to face the consequences of one's beliefs. You liberals want all America's benefits free."

"I haven't put a name to *you*," Kate said.

"I apologize. I ought not to have done so." And he bowed Kate from the room, urging her to visit his apartment whenever she chose. There would be someone there to let her in.

"I'm going for a walk first," Kate said, "or a bus ride. I'll go to your apartment later this afternoon, if that's all right. Perhaps we'll meet again."

"I shall be honored," Mr. Jablon said in his formal way. Kate noticed, with sorrow, the absence of tears or anger. He had found his defenses and taken his position securely behind them.

She decided to stroll about for a look at the houses wherein dwelt the members of her seminar. It was an excuse, really, for Kate loved prowling the streets and riding the buses and subways. Streethaunting, Kate called it, after Virginia Woolf's phrase, and she had been addicted to it all her life.

The Stark home, the Oliver home, the Kirkland home, the McCarthy home were all within walking distance of one another (or what Reed called Kate's idea of walking, which was anyone else's concept of a pilgrimage), but she had to take two buses to reach Morningside Heights. This was dangerous territory, Kate had heard, and she approached it with a certain wariness. Several uniformed guards patrolled the street, however. Kate, who liked to talk to people on jobs, stopped one and asked him what he was guarding.

"President's house," he said, pointing to a large redbrick building.

"The President of Columbia?" The man nodded.

"You never know when someone's going to take it into his head to stage a riot," he said. "Maybe their building's been torn down or something. Then there's the park thing."

Kate followed his glance across to Morningside Park, part of which had been leveled, apparently with a giant bulldozer. No trees, no rock outcroppings remained.

"What happened?" Kate asked.

"They were going to build a gymnasium." The man shrugged his shoulders.

Kate found that Irene Rexton's house was only a block or so down from the President's house, and she crossed over to it under the benevolent eye of the guard. The outer entrance was open, the inner door was locked; the lock was released only if a tenant pressed a button. Beyond, Kate was certain, was a self-service elevator. From the number of names on the directory, Kate concluded that there were two apartments to a floor, and only six floors. She pressed the button marked Rexton, but was hardly surprised to receive no answer. Irene was in school and the parents, one gathered, in Papua or somewhere. Or nearer to hand, perhaps, talking about Papua.

Kate wandered out again to talk to the guard. "Do you stay here in the evening too?" she asked.

"One of us does, in front of the President's house. Or just inside."

"Thank you," Kate said. She walked toward Broadway, and bought herself a hotdog, complete with sauerkraut and mustard, from a man with a cart. She walked down the street munching it, and looking no credit to the Theban, which frowned, ineffectually, upon its students eating on the street. Feeling by now walked out, Kate hailed a non-rush-hour taxi, and sank back to light a cigarette. She wondered if she had any stock in the company that made it, considered this for a while, and decided not to bother to find out. There was no question, living up to one's principles was very uphill work.

The taxi dropped Kate at a large building on Park Avenue, the Jablon address. Her taxi door was opened by a doorman who bounced out of the building eagerly and inquired, once he had placed her safely on the sidewalk, whom she wished to see.

"Mr. Jablon, whom I have just seen, is expecting me to call here," Kate said, with all the Fansler presence she could muster. The doorman directed her to the correct elevator, which she reached passing, by her count, three uniformed men on the way. She had planned to go upstairs and speak, or try to speak, to Angelica, descending when the evening shift would have come on, at which time she could question them about the night of Mrs. Jablon's death, or try to. Reed had pointed out that the police had been there before her, but Kate had read that policemen had IQs of 98, *average* she told Reed, appalled; imagine what some of them are.

"A hundred and thirty," Reed had answered. But Kate was not comforted.

The elevator man delivered her to the third floor, and waited until the door was open and Kate was admitted. A well-run building, with a well-run staff, Kate observed morosely. She had wildly hoped for negligence and confusion.

Kate explained her mission to the uniformed maid who opened the door for her. "But," Kate concluded, "I only want to see Angelica if she is quite happy to see me. If not, I shall go away until she feels better."

"If you will wait a minute, madam, I'll see." The maid allowed Kate to step inside and closed the door behind her. There were chairs in the large and formal foyer, but Kate stood. In a moment the maid passed through again, merely nodding at Kate, and was followed by a young man with long hair and beard, cut-off blue jeans and a distinctly regrettable shirt.

"You must be Miss Fansler," he announced, rubbing one extremely dirty foot against the other. "I'm Patrick Jablon." A Tom Sawyer with sex, was the immediate thought which flew into Kate's mind. "Angelica burst into tears again when she heard you were here, but from long experience I can tell they are tears of relief and gratitude. Ah, the patient herself."

An extremely damp and woebegone Angelica stood in the doorway, barefoot like her brother, but dressed in a long nightgown which looked as though it had been selected at a department store, not discovered in a rubbish heap.

"Hello," Kate said. "I've come to see how you are, and to talk to you. I've been walking around all day, and once I sit down I shall not get up again, probably for hours, so if you want me to go, please say so now rather than after I've put up my feet."

"You might as well come in," Angelica said. She started to lead the way toward her room and then apparently thought better of it. "Let's go in here," she said, leading the way toward the living room. "Would you like anything?" she asked, apparently reminded by the room's formality of some of the simpler laws of hospitality.

"As a matter of fact," Kate said, collapsing thankfully into a large lounge chair complete with ottoman, which she had been eying greedily from the foyer, "I'd love a cup of tea."

"I'll tell Nora," Angelica said. "Patrick will talk to you."

Patrick lay down on the floor, put his dirty feet up on the silk couch, and lit a cigarette, tossing the match at a distant ashtray which, inevitably, he missed.

"Do you smoke?" Patrick asked her.

Unsure any more what that question implied one's smoking *at*, Kate removed her own cigarettes from her purse and held them up in answer. She wriggled out of her coat, since no one had taken it from her, and leaning back, closed her eyes and put up her feet.

"Do you really want tea, or would you like Scotch or something? You don't have to stick with the tea just because you asked for it. We are all sufficiently impressed."

"Are Scotch and tea mutually exclusive?" Kate asked.

Patrick got to his feet and crossed to a beautifully equipped bar. "Ice?" he asked. Kate nodded. He brought the drink across to her, putting the glass, which had dribbled, down on a polished mahogany table. Kate lifted the glass immediately and wiped the table off. She then sipped the drink rather quickly, so as not to have seemed to be wiping up after him. But he was not deceived.

"All your generation drink," he announced.

"And all yours smell," Kate pleasantly said. "Cheers!"

Eleven

ANGELICA and the tea arrived together, the tea wheeled in on a tea tray with a silver teapot and everything handsome about it, Angelica in clothes which resembled her brother's, but were cleaner and rather less picturesque.

"Shall I pour you a cup of tea, madam?" the maid asked.

"Thank you," Kate said. "If I might have a cup, I'll help myself to the six or eight I intend to have afterward. No thank you, no cookies. I don't suppose you two will join me." Angelica shook her head; her brother did not trouble to answer. "Just sugar, thank you, no cream or lemon. Thank you very much."

Kate sipped the tea from the delicate teacup, and regarded the Jablons over its rim. She felt in no hurry, since they were unlikely to leave her until they had extracted from her, as they thought likely, all the information they could. One look had been sufficient to convince them that Kate was a source of information, certainly the best sort they were likely to come across for a while, and Kate was amused to realize how worried she had been about her welcome. Angelica, to do her justice, seemed glad that Kate had troubled to come out of personal interest, and said so.

"I was very concerned about you," Kate said, "and I did come to offer you some sort of comfort, if I could, though I felt convinced that you would find relief only in the truth, even if not expressed by the hitting of a mattress, or in dialogue with a pillow. Rather a good idea, that, I think; if you are forced to talk to someone, even a pillow standing in for someone, you get your thoughts and emotions into a certain order. Don't glare, dear; I'm quite serious."

"Someone's been talking to you." Angelica glowered.

"I am not a pariah," Kate pleasantly said. She watched a certain determined stubbornness pass over Angelica's face. It is not easy, when talking to a professional teacher more than twice your age, to learn more than you give away, and it was to the credit of Angelica's intelligence that she was aware of this.

"You know," Kate said, putting down her teacup and picking up her Scotch, "I came here prepared to ask a great many questions, not only of both of you, but perhaps of the servants as well and certainly of the elevator men."

"The elevator men?"

"Naturally. The question was, of course, how you got her out of the house without being seen. It's all very well for the police to question people, but we all know how overworked the police are even when doing their jobs, and it seemed unlikely that the staff here would admit to having been, say, involved in a poker game in the basement at the operative moment. I thought that some incisive questions and the gentle waving of ten-dollar bills might discover more than the police had. Do you mind if I get myself another cup of tea?" Since this question elicited no response whatever, Kate removed her feet from the ottoman and, rising, walked to the tea table to refill her cup. "Perhaps I can push it nearer, to save steps," she said, suiting the action to the words. She put a teaspoon of sugar in the tea, stirred it, sat down again, and put up her legs.

"Look," Patrick said.

"No," Kate said, "you listen. Where was I?"

"You had just determined to bribe the elevator man to get the evidence you wanted."

"Crudely put, but accurate. I have, however, unde-termined, which saves my character for the moment, not to mention my money. Because of course she wasn't removed from here; she couldn't have been. Not after I saw how this building works. A different set of men, of course, but run strictly and on the best old-fashioned principles. Did you say something?"

Patrick had, some fatigued obscenity, but he did not choose to repeat it.

"As to the other girls, they each live in a house of the same sort as this, not quite so stiff in its manner, per-haps, but unlikely to find itself with a wholly deserted lobby at ten o'clock in the evening or, shall we say, nine-thirty. I had planned also to ask you a great many questions, if you would allow me, and a few pointed ones if you wouldn't, but I've changed my mind. I'm not going to ask you anything. I'm going to tell you something instead. All right?"

"Miss Fansler," Angelica said, "I haven't been feeling very well. In fact, I just got back from the hospital and . . ."

"Yes, my dear, as Miss Tyringham would say. And I thought it very wise of you to go to the hospital, murmuring incoherently under sedation, having hysterics, in short, refusing to say anything at all. It was certainly understandable that you would be feeling awful. There are not many people who are absolutely better off dead, but I'm afraid your mother may have been such a person. Does that sound frightful? It was meant to. My version of mattress hitting and pillow talking. Though when people we have wished dead die, we have to try a little harder not to dive straight down a well of remorse, particularly if we've killed them."

"This is blackmail," Patrick said.

"Yes, it is, rather. Because, if you don't listen to the story, someone else may, and that could be disturbing since you don't know yet what the story is. When I've finished it, however, if you want me to, I will simply leave. I am like your grandfather in this, if in nothing else: If I give you my word, I will keep it. Terrible as he made you feel, if he told you that he would do something in two hours, you would believe, would you not, that indeed he would keep his word?"

"O.K., you've made your point. No doubt the two of you share all the same honorable attitudes. You've probably already been to see him?"

"I have, as a matter of fact. I've just come from his office, well, a few hours ago anyway; I asked his permission to come here and see you, and we talked about

Vietnam and one or two other things. We don't see eye to eye on any of them, not a single one, but I was reminded of duels in the age of chivalry when there were agreed-upon rules, and one abided by them. I think your grandfather is mistaken, but that is neither here nor there. Mrs. Banister could probably handle this best, but for certain reasons . . ."

Kate, looking down at the brother and sister, both regarding her with looks unpleasantly compounded of distrust, curiosity, and disdain, was reminded of Miss Tyringham's class in ethics, the results of the questionnaire. Clearly, Kate told herself, I can't do anything right, but I can at least not be accused of hypocrisy.

"Mrs. Banister hasn't got anything to do with it," Angelica said.

"With what?" Kate asked. She raised her eyes to meet Angelica's.

"Oh, cool it, Angie," Patrick said.

"Sorry," Kate said. "Believe it or not, I'm trying like hell to be straightforward and simple, in fact, I'm oozing sincerity from every pore, but I sound as though I were leading you up the garden path. Why is communication so bloody difficult?"

"Because you're trying to find something out," Patrick said. "You're manipulative."

"Oh, balderdash," Kate said. "I beg your pardon. Back to the beginning, one step after another, stop me if I set a foot off the line, that is, if you care about the truth at all. You always say you do, your generation. I sometimes wonder if there *are* such things as generations. It's like talking about all women, all men, all children—nonsense, really. Here we go."

But what am I doing here, Kate thought; groping

through the clouds of human misery to reach two adolescents who have learned with reason, that little in life is what it purports to be? Yet I do feel that directness is our only hope, looking things in the face and not dropping our eyes. We would no doubt do much better at Esalen, naked before the setting sun or half immersed in sulphur baths—Kate, casting about for information among various acquaintances, had found sunsets and nude surphur baths figuring prominently in all accounts. A pillow, a mattress, an involved audience—well, one could scarcely fly to Esalen or arrange an encounter session every time an educational crisis reared its head these uncertain days. For a moment Kate tried to picture herself naked in a sulphur bath (tubs? mud? like a swimming pool?) and gave it up.

"Angelica," Kate began, "and her friends, both from Mrs. Banister's drama group and, by extension, from the *Antigone* seminar, began in a mild sort of way holding what we will call encounter groups. These started, I believe, not as ways to work out personal problems, but as devices to encourage students to throw themselves into dramatic situations, and to undertake dramatic expression. Because of the seminar, I guess, these more or less informal groups began to act out the *Antigone*. It is, of course, a play remarkably relevant— if you will excuse the expression—to our life today, and, because of Patrick, it soon became particularly relevant to the situation of the Jablons." Kate saw the two of them color; Patrick looked down and began picking at a dirty toe; Angelica bit her lip. Don't cry, Kate silently prayed; not yet.

"I don't mean, of course, that there is any parallel between the characters in the *Antigone* and the members of the Jablon family, but certain resemblances do strike one with overwhelming force. Creon, for example, says so many things which seem to echo in the voice of your grandfather: 'Nor would I ever dream the country's foe a friend to myself.' 'If any makes a friend of more account than his fatherland, that man hath no place in my regard.' 'Disobedience is the worst of evils. This it is that ruins cities, that makes homes desolate.' I could go on; we all could. But the question he seems to me to have been asking about you, Patrick, is also a question of Creon's: 'Men of my age—are we indeed to be schooled, then, by men of his?' I think, slowly, painfully, he has begun to learn that the answer to that question may have to be yes. I think we have all begun to learn, even from Angelica, who has, like Antigone, 'a hot heart for chilling deeds.' "

She had their attention now. She felt, indeed, rather like Antigone herself, to whom Ismene wisely said: "A hopeless quest should not be made at all." Was this quest hopeless? No, Ismene was not wise, for the only hopeless quests are those we fail to dare.

"I think," Kate went on, "that the encounter sessions slipped, imperceptibly at first, from dramatic renderings of the *Antigone* to actual dramatizations, with pillow and mattress, of Angelica's difficult family situation. Perhaps others also had encounter sessions, I don't know and it doesn't really matter. What I feel certain of is that Mrs. Banister found herself in a soul-rending dilemma, if you will allow my generation its unfortunate tendency to hyperbole. In a sense, the group had gone too far; certainly it had already long exceeded the expectations of the Theban in setting up a drama group. There was always danger, in such a situation, that some real emotional problem would come up, a problem which only the most experienced of group leaders (as I believe they call them at Esalen) would know how to handle. If she reproved the group for its activities and deserted it, she would certainly save her own skin, that is, her job and immediate sense of responsibility, but she would leave several adolescent girls, who she had every reason to think would continue their encounter groups without her, in real danger. She decided, and greatly to her credit, to remain with the group, even in its meetings outside the school, and to hope that she might dissipate the energy of the sessions, particularly with the coming of spring and the light turning of young fancies to love.

"Unfortunately, her excellent plan was not allowed to wend its intelligent way. The other evening," Kate sipped her tea, "I'm certain you know to which evening I refer . . ."

"Is this all really supposed to be helping us?" Patrick asked. "Is that what you're telling yourself, or are you just enjoying sitting there, holding forth?"

Kate looked at him. " 'A youthful mind, when stung, is fierce.' That's another quote from the *Antigone*, though God knows it needs not Sophocles to tell us this. I like to hold forth, I'm an aging, long-winded, pontificating old bore, but if you think this is my idea of fun and games, think again. Frankly, I'd rather be smoking pot at Woodstock on an overcrowded field in the rain with everyone singing rock, which, in case you miss the allusion, is as near to hell as I can imagine. Still," Kate was suddenly revolted at the way she was forcing herself on these two, "perhaps you're right. If I have to tell the damn story to someone, and I'm afraid

I do, I suppose it might as well be Miss Tyringham. I've always said that shifting problems is the first rule for a long and pleasant life, and anyway it is rightfully her problem. She'll have to know it all before long. I'm sorry. We all do believe, and I more than most, that our inherent honesty and good intentions will somehow be perfectly clear to anyone we care for. It is the result in my case of being the youngest and most indulged child in the family."

With a sigh of relief (no one can say I didn't try) Kate again lifted her feet from the ottoman and arose. She picked up coat and purse, deliberated whether or not to request to be led to a ladies' room, and decided against it. Not quite rush hour, maybe a taxi, Reed, and a home whose doorstep, so help me God, she thought, no one under thirty will ever darken again. As to the seminar and the Theban, these would in time dwindle away from sight.

"Thank you for the tea," Kate said, "Forgive me. I have been suffering from hubris; the Greeks, as always, had a word for it. My whole generation," she turned to Patrick, "thanks you for the Scotch."

Now it is one of the more appalling if unarguable aspects of human nature that we only become overwhelmingly attractive to certain people when we have learned to feel indifference for them, or even scorn. Your employer will always want to keep you if someone has offered you another job you very much want to take. A spouse is never so attractive as when desired by another. Furthermore, if we have just determined never to bother seeing someone again, it is unaccountably annoying to be told by him that he has no further use for our company. Kate had wanted to know the two young Jablons, but it was her sincere dismissal of them which now betrayed her unquestionably into their affairs.

"Apologies," Patrick said. "Heartfelt. I will get you more Scotch. I will wash my feet. I will put on a tie—no, I won't put on a tie; I suppose you know all about that too. I will stand up because you are a lady." He leapt gracefully, with the heartbreaking grace of young men, to his feet.

"Naturally you're sick of me," Angelica said. "Everyone is. Patrick was the only one I even *dreamed* I could help, and he was attacked by dogs. 'A corpse for dogs to eat.' That's a quotation too." And Angelica began noisily to weep.

"I was *not* attacked by dogs; I just thought I would be. And I am not a corpse. Miss Fansler, please stay. Think about commitment, have more tea."

"Oh, God," Kate said. "Hell, sin, and corruption. Why do I always think the truth will be easy? And, if you tell me my generation always thinks that, I promise you I will spit."

"More ice?" Patrick asked. "Angelica, stop crying and get Miss Fansler some ice. I'll take the tea tray back before it's called for. What sign were you born under?" he asked Kate, hands on the tea table.

"Keep Out," Kate said, "and I still haven't read it properly."

After a while, they reassembled themselves. Patrick had got rid of the tea tray and put on some sneakers, which, while not much cleaner than his feet, were not feet and therefore preferable. Kate had accepted another drink and, having decided on the ladies' room after all, had been and returned. Angelica had blown her nose in a final sort of way. Why is it, Kate thought, that human love breathes only where there is emotion? How much better to be the old men in Plato's *Republic*. She sipped from her Scotch and continued, as though no interruption had been.

"The other evening, the night your mother died, the group had decided to have an encounter session. Freemond Oliver had come here first to dinner with Angelica; you were to go later to Irene Rexton's house for the session. The others all met there, though I am uncertain how many of you there were. When Freemond and Angelica left, Patrick remained at home with his mother, anyway for a time; Mr. Jablon had gone out earlier to play bridge.

"I assumed, at first, that the session had taken place here, but I now see that that is unlikely. For one thing, Angelica would have been unlikely to want to risk being overheard by her mother and grandfather. However, I only realized that afterward, when I had been trying to discover a home with no adults likely to be around, with a lobby free of attendants.

"What happened here after Angelica and Freemond left I am less certain of. Let me guess. Your mother became distressed about something and demanded from you," Kate nodded at Patrick, "where Angelica had gone."

" 'Became distressed about something' is good," Patrick said. "She never knew anything as simple as distress; she started at the top of her lungs and then got shriller."

Kate could imagine it, and the weariness these youngsters felt for their mother. They must have passed through fear of upsetting her, through intermittent and even more intermittent affection, to impatience, a terrible pity, and, finally, indifference. Her being dead could not change that; she was more recently dead than their feeling for her.

"I was in my room, listening to Dylan and the ball game and sort of looking at *Catch-22*, I'd already read it, when she stormed in. No knocking, nothing. I heard her over Dylan and Phil Rizzuto and the fans cheering in the background. They must have heard her in Battery Park." Patrick paused a moment, as though remembering her again with an unhappy vividness. "I won't try to repeat her words, or her tone, but the general purport was that everyone had gone out, no one considered her, Angelica had *not* asked her permission, did I know where she had gone, it would never occur to 'your grandfather' to play bridge with *her*, et cetera, and so on. I'm sure you know the sort of thing. She finally demanded if I knew where Angelica had gone, had a great deal to say about my knowing and her not knowing, and ended up by demanding to be taken there."

Patrick paused and looked about him for a cigarette. Kate offered him one of hers, which he took with a smile and a nod of thanks. It was clear that Patrick had immense possibilities for charm, given half a chance. He looked rather like his stern grandfather, though the grimness came from tensions much harder to bear than the necessity to earn one's living and support one's family, or so Kate, who had never had to do either, supposed.

"You know all about it," Patrick said, smiling. "You go on."

"She talked you into going up there, didn't she? But demanded that you first put on a tie."

"I said you knew all about it. I got into a shirt finally, because it seemed easier than arguing with her—she never listened, anyway, and never heard or wanted to—but when I put on my *most* conservative tie, a white design on a sort of green, she objected violently that I looked like a hippie, her general word for anyone who isn't dressed by Saks Fifth Avenue."

"Well," Angelica interjected, "that tie does look like psychedelic spermatozoa on a background of . . ."

"All *right*," Patrick said, "we get the picture." But he was clearly glad to see Angelica trying, at any rate, for lightness, and they all grinned pleasantly at one another. "Soooo, as Angie would say, she went into Granddad's room and got me one of his ties, which of course he would have hated her doing, but it's not often you can irritate two people with one small gesture. She insisted on tying it for me, which I loathe having her, or anyone, do and . . ."

"The label came off as she tied it. She seems to have stuck it in her pocket and gone on."

"Yes, that's like her. She was compulsively neat. I mean, you can't imagine. She was forever picking things up off the floor, even things that weren't there. And complaining about how terribly things were cleaned, how spoiled the servants were, and how no one wanted to work any more—she, of course, not having done any work in the last quarter century."

"I'm surprised the servants stayed," Kate said.

"Well, Granddad treats them very well, and gives them lavish presents and all; they adore him, of course; it seems to be part of the servant mentality or something. He claims that his definition of a liberal is a man who worries about everyone but his wife and servants, so you see it's all part of the general picture. She did look around for a wastepaper basket which wasn't there because I'd used it for shooting baskets into and the bottom came out, and she worried on about that for a while and must have finally stuck the thing in her pocket. Well, we got there, taking a taxi with her telling the driver not to go over ten miles an hour or something, God it was awful, and then clinging to me because the driver would stop and rape her if I took my eyes off him for a minute, and then, of course, Morningside Drive."

"Well, she wasn't far wrong about Morningside Drive."

"Probably not, but we actually made it to the Rexton apartment without being attacked."

"I still don't see," Angelica said, "why you didn't talk her out of it, or just refuse to come. Why bring her there, I mean what was the *point*?" Angelica began to sound weepy again, and Patrick answered her in loud tones, which he clearly hoped would pull her back from another bout.

"For God's sake, Angie, let's be honest and cut out the crap. I went partly because she made such a hell of a thing about it, but also because I wanted to see what went on in those sessions of yours. O.K., I was curious . . ."

"But to let her go there. You *knew* she wouldn't have gone without you, she . . ."

"Cool it, Angie, just cool it. I went, it's over, cut the goddamn crap." He got up and started walking around the room, stopping with his back to Kate, to glare at

Angie. Apparently the look spoke more clearly than his words, for Angelica was silent.

"That's all there is to the story," Patrick said, turning around. "It all goes bang like a burst balloon. She looked around the Rexton apartment, which was just a home, you know, chairs to sit on, lamps to read by, and not the smallest interest in taste or impressing anyone, I mean, not a status symbol in sight or the least likelihood of anybody saying, 'Oh, what an *interesting* room, who *is* your decorator, you did it *yourself*, you ought to go into the decorating business, you're *thinking* of it, well I'll be your first customer.' " Patrick was a good mimic, and they all laughed. "It was just a home where people lived and were happy and she turned her nose up at it, naturally, or rather, she never did anything naturally, she just turned up her nose. Then she said, 'Patrick, I want to see where you hid out in that school,' so I took her over there, in another taxi, and she kind of mingled with the parents who were there having some sort of meeting, and I lost track of her, and I suppose I should have waited but I didn't, I came home, and Angie was home, and I guess she just died from seeing those dogs. Believe me, it's more than possible. I know, having seen them, and I *like* dogs."

"Taxi drivers can be traced, you know," Kate said.

"Sometimes, but it doesn't prove a negative. I mean, if a driver says he took so-and-so from here to there, and has it on his sheet, he did, but if no driver can be found, that doesn't mean he doesn't exist, if you follow me."

Kate let it go for the moment.

"Who was at the session when you arrived?" she asked.

Patrick shrugged his shoulders. "Haven't a clue," he said. "You know, the usual bunch of Angie's friends, a bunch of creeps, really." He smiled at Angie.

"One's sister's friends always are, I assume. Who was there, Angelica?"

Angelica stopped to consider. Poor kid, Kate thought. She is trying to fit her story in with Patrick's, and to protect—whom?—and yet to tell as much of the truth as she safely can, since she is bright enough to know that the more you can stick to the truth, the easier it is to lie in a coherent and sustained way.

"Irene," she said, "and Freemond and me, and Elizabeth. Elizabeth worked rather well in those sessions, though we never thought she would. There were only the four of us."

"No one else from the drama group, or Betsy, or Alice Kirkland?"

"No, it really was a kind of private session, about me—well, all of us," she hastily added. "Alice is kind of, well . . ."

"I know," Kate said, "though I have hopes. Why not Betsy?"

"Well, for one thing, her father carries on like a raving maniac if she goes out at night, so . . ."

Kate nodded. She doubted that was the only reason. Betsy's tongue was sharp, and, scorning tact, which she recognized as frequently more insulting than an insult, she also, like many sensitive people, had no concept of how cruel her own words could be. It was an irony Kate had noticed often. Still, all the girls had been present at most of the sessions, as the unwary revelations in the seminar indicated. It had been Alice, of course, who had given the show away.

"Did you decide to work out something special that night?" Kate asked.

"Well, yes," Angelica said. "I was trying to express my feelings about my mother. . . ." Her voice trailed unhappily away.

"Wasn't Mrs. Banister there?"

"No," Angelica answered, with a forthrightness always recognizable in someone who has been lying and can at last tell the simple truth. "We didn't tell her about it. For one thing, we'd been taking up an awful lot of her time, and then, it wasn't a real session, you see, with only four of us." She stopped talking, and her voice died away in the room.

Kate leaned back in the chair and closed her eyes. She was not very good at this sort of thing and, as a result, she had got herself into exactly the sort of corner she had hoped to avoid. She believed that she had the truth about the session up until the arrival of Patrick and his mother. The four girls had been alone in the Rexton apartment having an encounter session. But Patrick, she was certain, had not gone with his mother to the school—not only was the mother's agreeing to any such thing, let alone suggesting it, absolutely beyond the bounds of possibility, but Kate knew, as Patrick did not, that the mother could not have been killed by the dogs.

They still believed Kate to know more than she had revealed, but they weren't giving anything away. Why should they? And what after all did Kate know? One fact, that was all she had left.

Mrs. Jablon had been dead when the dogs found her. It was the only conceivable explanation of the dogs' not stopping when they came across her, of her body's being found next morning, in a state of rigor mortis. She had died—where?—and her body had been brought to the school and deposited there. The dogs do not stop for the dead. Reed had made a point of asking Mr. O'Hara.

How had Mrs. Jablon got to the school?

Suppose she had, as Patrick suggested, gone to school, whether for the reason he had offered or for others, had walked upstairs, and died from a heart attack there in the art room? Would such a fearful woman walk up to a floor where no one was, to die in a deserted art studio? Certainly she would not have taken the elevator alone, being scared of that sort of thing and, from what Kate could gather, unlikely to be able to operate any mechanical device, however simple. Suppose Mr. O'Hara had taken her up, thinking she was a parent, and she had walked down to the art room? But surely someone at the meeting, teacher or parent, would have seen her. All the inquiries the police had made established the fact that no one had seen her, and Mr. O'Hara, who had seen her dead body, swore he had never laid eyes on her before, certainly hadn't taken her up in the elevator.

Without a doubt the blasted woman was dead when she was brought to the Theban.

Why was she brought to the Theban?

That was the point, of course. Well, what are you to do with a body? It's the most difficult part of murders, as detective novelists are always pointing out. There had so recently been the case of Patrick and the dogs to stand as a suggestion. But who knew about Patrick and the dogs? Unlike the discovery of Mrs. Jablon's body, this event had not become general news. Could it have been someone within the Theban? It was unthinkable that Julia or Miss Tyringham would have involved the Theban. Surely their efforts, had they been there, would have been quite the opposite—to get the body as far from the school as possible, always supposing one could imagine either of them moving bodies in the first place.

Which, when you came to think of it, was the point. Why had the body been moved, and how?

To begin with, where had Mrs. Jablon died? She had not died at home—her second exit, carried or under her own steam, would have been observed in this lobby. But her exit, dead or alive, from the Rexton home would have been seen by no one, not even the guard outside the President's house. He was more than likely inside; well, he at least could be questioned. And Morningside Drive was considered so dangerous that the streets were almost guaranteed to be deserted.

"I know," Kate said, hoping she sounded as though she did, "that your mother died at the Rexton home. Was she frightened to death, or did she scream herself into the next world in a fit of temper?"

Angelica and Patrick looked at Kate, and then at each other. Her momentary silence—it had been little longer than that—as she sat with her eyes closed, had encouraged them. The worst perhaps was over, the last river safely forded. They, who had expected a truce, again girded themselves for battle.

Patrick shrugged and looked at his sister.

"It isn't a bit probable, you know," Kate said, "that the woman your mother has been pictured to be would want to see where you had been frightened—she would be likelier, from all reports, to avoid the place at all costs—or would allow herself to be alone there for a single moment. Going to the school at night was at best unbelievable, but for her . . ."

"It's no good, Patrick," Angelica said. "You're right, of course. Mother died at Irene's. I was talking to her, pretending the pillow was her, when she came in. She and Patrick just stood there listening. It wasn't Patrick's fault—I guess he was as thunderstruck as Mother, though not in the same way."

"But surely they rang the buzzer downstairs, not to mention the apartment door."

"We didn't," Patrick said. "There was someone going in at the time with a key, and we went in with him."

"That can be checked out, anyway," Kate said. "There aren't many tenants in the house—so that's a step forward. I've been to the house, you see," she added. "What sort of man was he?"

"Just a man, about your age. A professor, probably. He went to a higher floor. The apartment door was open, unlocked. My mother just sort of burst in—well, that *was* her way; she liked sudden confrontations with her children."

"And she got one, beyond her wildest dreams. A confrontation with herself, too. You were telling the pillow exactly how you felt, had always felt, and felt now?" Angelica nodded. "She had no business to be there," Kate said. "But why did Irene leave the door open, in such a neighborhood?"

"Irene said her parents could never remember their keys. Besides, there was usually someone staying there who didn't have a key and would arrive at any moment. It's that kind of household."

"I see. So she heard you and dropped dead?"

"Not quite." Angelica looked at Patrick.

"If I'd thought she was hysterical in my room," he said, "I hadn't known from hysterical. She started screeching about all she'd done for Angelica, given her her whole life, been so generous. She kicked the pillow out of the way and smacked Angie—it was gross." Patrick lit another cigarette. "And then, well, she paused a second, to draw breath I guess, and Angie said, in a quiet voice, 'What have you ever done for me?' And Irene, who looks like an angel of the Lord anyway, said, 'Mrs. Jablon, what have you ever done for Angelica except make her feel unwanted? Why don't you . . .' That was as far as Irene got, because Mother—well, she sort of fell back into a chair, and we rushed up and said, 'Can we get anything?' and someone went for water, and Irene said, 'I better call a doctor,' and she did go to the phone, but she got the doctor's exchange, which said, 'Hold on,' and then went off the line, you know the way they always do, and then—well, she was dead. There wasn't any question about that."

"I see," Kate said. It seemed to be her line for the day.

"And then," Patrick concluded, "we saw we had a problem. I realize now the sensible thing would have been to call a doctor and let it go at that. But it *did* seem that Angie had killed her, and there would be all sorts of terrible questions, and we couldn't just leave her there with Irene, and once an ambulance came it would all be investigated, so . . ."

"Someone remembered Patrick's experience at the Theban," Angelica said, "well, it was me, actually, so Patrick carried her there."

"That's it," Patrick said in a final sort of way. "That's the whole story."

"You carried a dead woman through the streets from way uptown on Morningside Drive to the East Seventies?"

"No. I stole a car."

"You did?"

"Yes. I simply broke into a car in front of the house and took it. Later I returned it. The parking space was gone, of course, but I left it double parked. I guess the owner found it all right."

"How do you steal a car?"

"Oh, you reach underneath the hood and connect some wires; it's done all the time. I read somewhere that the automobile companies are working on a device to prevent it."

Kate wanted to ask him for more details about the wires, but she simply could not find the brutal energy to pursue the point.

"She just sort of sat up on the seat next to me," Patrick said.

There was a silence, to which they all listened for a time.

"Well, Angelica," Kate said. "I see why you didn't want to talk about it, but all those reasons, or most of them, are finished now. I think the thing to do is to talk it out. Will you tell Miss Tyringham about it? Between you, you have caused her school a good deal of trouble, and it seems only fair that she should know the truth. Besides, I think she'll understand. Apart from everything else, she has met your mother. And your grandfather; I think you should tell him too. What he now suspects is probably not too far from the truth, but the truth is always preferable to an unhappy fantasy. Will you talk to them?"

"Could you tell them? Miss Tyringham, anyway?"

"I could. Will you settle for some minor blackmail? I'll speak to Miss Tyringham, if you'll return to school and try to take up your life again. As to Patrick, who acted the best way he could, under the circumstances, his major problems are still with his draft board."

"Angie stood by me. It wasn't her fault the dogs were there. Only those damn dogs nearly scared the hell out of me when I didn't expect them, and failed when we were counting on them—ungrateful beasts. I think she's right, Angie. Finish up at the Theban, and try to work it out now. After all, we are free of her, however unfilial it sounds to say so."

"I'll expect you in class Monday," Kate said. "You might let Irene and Freemond and Elizabeth know it's all right, and—no more encounter sessions without a qualified leader. Will you agree to that?"

They got up, nodding eagerly. They would have agreed to anything.

Kate was soaking in a hot tub with her eyes closed when Reed came in.

"You would have been proud of me," she said. "I walked miles and miles and solved the mystery. Only I don't know what to do next."

"There's always nothing," Reed said hopefully. "Do you want a martini in here, or can you make it to the living room?"

"Actually, I've been having Scotch and tea all afternoon. Are you busy this evening?"

"You mean, after my martini? I'm at your command—no, I retract that, but I'll admit, cautiously, to being free if you promise that you aren't making *plans*."

"All right," Kate said. "I'll go alone. You faced the dogs alone."

Reed, who had been leaving the bathroom, returned. "Where are you going?" he asked. "I don't want to know but tell me anyway."

"Oh, get your martini. I'll be there in a minute. Why does my generation always admire loyalty?"

"What kind of 'tea' was it?" Reed asked. Kate noisily turned on the water.

But when they called her, she said she would come to see them. Her husband had to get somewhere, and would drop her off. "Don't worry," she said on the phone, "I shan't funk it or run out on you. I'm glad it's come out, actually. I despise deception."

"Don't say anything to anyone before you talk to us," Kate said. "Because, you see, it hasn't yet come out at all."

"All right. Keep cool."

She arrived shortly, somewhat breathless, and shook Reed's hand vigorously on being introduced. She had that enormous energy frequently found in small women, and the downright opinions more usually found in large ones.

"Did you come on the motorcycle?" Kate asked.

"Oh, yes. Do you think it unfeeling of me? I regard all superstitions and shibboleths as greatly dangerous; besides, I hardly knew the woman and disliked intensely what I'd heard of her. Who talked?"

"About you, no one. Everybody was a positive monument of discretion about protecting everybody else."

"What will you drink, Mrs. Banister?" Reed asked.

"Oh, just a glass of cold water, if you have it. I don't drink. Always feel good enough without it, I guess."

"One of the things I like about New York," Reed said, "is that people feel they have to apologize for not drinking." He poured the glass of water and handed it to her.

Kate took up her tale. "I got most of the story out of Angelica and Patrick this afternoon, by means I'm not entirely happy to think about. But while they came through with the truth—I'm pretty certain it's the truth, and, anyway, it can be checked—about everything through the death of that unfortunate woman, their story was pure fantasy from then on. Patrick had to pretend he knew how to steal a car, when he knew exactly as much about it as I did, having read the same journalism. They wanted to protect you, you see. I'm afraid I'm hopelessly old-fashioned and admire that."

"I'm glad you do. People just don't realize how beautiful these young people are. They seem to prefer some status-happy youth in the proper clothes with one foot in the suburbs and the other in a prestigious college. Of course, the Jablons are a special problem, and then there is this terrible war. I'm glad they called me when they needed help. It was I who thought of the school; that's what bothers me. I remembered about Patrick, as soon as I got to the Rextons', and I thought, Aha, let the dogs scare someone else to death. And it would have worked, you know, if that beastly man hadn't been so damn pig-headed about his nasty animals."

"*Or* if guard dogs were trained to stop for dead bodies. Unlike us, you know, dogs can tell, immediately and indisputably."

"I call that sinister. Well, it was a jolly good plan all the same, particularly since we thought of it on the spur of the moment."

"At least you had Patrick to help you, which must have . . ."

"To help me what?"

"Get her on the motorcycle and all. Didn't he?"

Mrs. Banister sipped her water. "Oh, I see," she said. "You assumed it had to be Patrick who helped. An interesting example of socially bred female humility."

"You don't mean it was Angelica?"

"No, I don't. After all, she *was* their mother, inadequate and destructive as she may have been, and handling dead bodies is disturbing under ideal circumstances, if there are ideal circumstances for handling dead bodies, even if she isn't one's mother. It was Irene who helped me."

"Irene!"

"Certainly. She said that these days there must be no more Ismenes."

Kate stared at her. "You," Kate said to Reed, "have not seen Irene. Though I can't imagine why I think that has anything to do with it. After all, her parents . . ."

"One must *never* characterize people," Mrs. Banister said, bouncing up to get herself another glass of water ("I drink twelve a day," she said. "It keeps the system flushed out"); she waved Reed away as he rose to help her. "I am capable of pouring a glass of water, thank you. Elizabeth and Angelica and Patrick and Freemond went home; the Jablons dropped Elizabeth and Freemond on the way. Irene and I carried down the body after they had gone. I thought, least involved, soonest mended. Of course, we had to keep a look-out, but only till we got out of the building. I'd parked the motorcycle right outside it—it was fortunately not a night when Andrew needed it, since it would have been more uphill work on the bicycle, though we would have managed, have no fear of that—and we slid her onto the pillion and I got on front and started it. Irene sat in the back, and we held her up between us. Fortunately, I had two extra helmets, which I always carry, so we weren't stopped for that, and the helmet helped to disguise the fact that she wasn't exactly holding her head up. I'm sure it's the only time the poor woman ever rode on a motorcycle; I understand she was phobic." Mrs. Banister paused to sip her water, while Kate and Reed avoided each other's eyes.

"I had her arms tied around my waist with my rain-coat belt, and Irene held her up. *Fortunately*, when we got to the school there was no one about—there never are people on that street, but I knew there was a meeting and thought the parents might be leaving. Thank God we were early enough, and we wheeled her inside, right on the motorcycle, and hid her on the dolly with the dust cloth, the canvas thing, over her. To tell you the truth, I thought we might have to drag her down to the lower floor, but when I got back from parking the motorcycle, the chauffeurs had started to arrive, and the watchman was out there talking with them. Have you read *Men in Groups* by Lionel Tiger, a wildly male-chauvinist book?"

Kate and Reed shook their heads.

"You ought to. Clearly O'Hara is only happy in the

company of men and couldn't resist the chauffeurs; lucky for us, anyway. I trundled her right across the lobby, under the canvas, of course—I'd made Irene go out and wait for me in a drugstore on the corner, by the way, I didn't need her any more—and I just popped into the elevator, drove to the third floor, popped her out onto the art-room floor, where I *thought* the dogs couldn't help noticing her."

"That was fortunate, or Mr. O'Hara might not have found her in the morning," Reed said. "You dropped her right across from the alarm."

"I realized that, later. The room was easiest because it had a slightly wider doorway. Then I took the dolly back down."

"Why? Wouldn't it have been easier to leave it?" Kate asked.

"Certainly it would have been *easier*, but I didn't want anyone to associate her with the dolly. She was supposed to have come in under her own power, so to speak. I didn't want them to think of the dolly at all, so the best thing was to return it to its place. O'Hara was still being a man in a happy male group and I hurried out of the building with scarcely a glance from him. Doubtless he thought to himself, A mother who walked down, do her good, and sneered, if he saw me at all, which I doubt; his back was to me. I ran round and picked up the motorcycle, gathered up Irene, and off we went. I dropped her home, and found, when I got back, that Andrew was still shut up in his studio, working, and that I'd got hungry from all the extra wear and tear on the tissue, so I had an apple and nut salad. Anything else you want to know? Thirsty business, explaining." She quaffed her water.

Kate and Reed were speechless. Reed began slowly to grin. Kate glared at him.

"There is still the problem of telling the school. Miss Tyringham, at any rate," she said.

"Yes," Mrs. Banister agreed. "No doubt I will be bounced."

"Well, from her point of view, of course, it does seem that you didn't have the good of the school at heart in quite the way the Theban expects from its faculty."

"Probably I don't," Mrs. Banister said frankly. "It's rather too structured a school for my tastes, anyhow. You don't think she'll try to interfere with my finding work elsewhere?"

"Oh, no, I think that's most unlikely. I'm not even sure she won't want you back. When I asked her about her attitude toward a faculty member involved . . ."

"Did you suspect me?"

"Not of providing transport, no. I had come to expect it was at the encounter group that whatever happened happened, but, frankly, I assumed you had been there. Angelica said you hadn't been with such transparent truthfulness that I dismissed it. But what she said was that you hadn't been included in the group for the evening. She didn't say you didn't come later."

"One had to rally round. Well, I'm giving up the motorcycle."

"Are you?"

"Andrew and I have agreed; starting next spring it will be only bicycles and shanks' mare. Less pollution, less noise, less hurry, and good for the muscles and general health. Thank you for your honesty," Mrs. Banister said, bouncing into the hall and seizing her helmet.

"Thank you," Kate and Reed said, shaking hands as though, Reed said to Kate when she had gone, the visit had been for the purpose of closing a mutually beneficial deal.

"But it was," Kate said. She walked to the phone to tell Miss Tyringham that she would have a good deal to report in the morning. Eight o'clock at the Theban? Yes, Kate guessed she could make it.

"You might as well give me the song program for the shower now," Kate said. "I'll be joining you."

April sobbed and flirted its way into May. The Theban, a century old, endured. Miss Tyringham talked slightly less of retiring to her cottage in England. Julia spoke as though the curriculum might soon achieve revision. The *Antigone* seminar argued its way into many wider questions. Mr. Jablon sent Kate a short, noncommittal, unemotional acknowledgment of her efforts.

Up on the roof, Lily and Rose slept away the days.

THE PUZZLED HEART

by

AMANDA CROSS

"Cross again displays her virtuosity,
wit and keen intelligence in this
vintage performance. . ."
—*Houston Chronicle*

"What makes this book a delight is the
literate dialogue. . ."
—*Los Angeles Times*

Published by Ballantine Books.
Available at your local bookstore.

Recently re-designed
with beautiful new covers

Look for these
AMANDA CROSS
classics:

IN THE LAST ANALYSIS
The First Kate Fansler Mystery

and

POETIC JUSTICE

From the master of the American literary
mystery come these short stories—
including eight mysteries featuring
Kate Fansler:

❋ ❋ ❋

AMANDA CROSS

THE COLLECTED STORIES

❋ ❋ ❋

A *People* "Page-Turner of the Week"

"For more than twenty-five years,
Amanda Cross has been blazing a trail
for the rest of us to follow."

—Sara Paretsky

Available in trade paperback from
Ballantine Books.

Be sure to read the complete collection of
AMANDA CROSS mysteries:

IN THE LAST ANALYSIS

THE JAMES JOYCE MURDER

POETIC JUSTICE

THE THEBAN MYSTERIES

THE QUESTION OF MAX

DEATH IN A TENURED POSITION

SWEET DEATH, KIND DEATH

NO WORD FROM WINIFRED

A TRAP FOR FOOLS

THE PLAYERS COME AGAIN

AN IMPERFECT SPY

THE PUZZLED HEART

HONEST DOUBT

Published by Ballantine Books.
Available at your local bookstore.